I0622293

# .40 Cal:

### "Her nephew was killed with one; and she didn't like it!!

## Saint Santa Fe

.40 Cal: "Her nephew was killed with one; and she didn't like it !!

ISBN: 978-1-7377252-0-6  (Paperback)
ISBN: 978-1-7377252-1-3  (Hardcover)
Library of Congress Control Number: 2021917461

Any references to historical events, real people, or real places are used fictitiously. Names, characters, and places are products of the author's imagination.

Front cover image by Saint Santa Fe
First printing edition 2021

EloKim Publishing
EloKimPublishingLLLP@Gmail.Com

# 1st Quarter

## Work hard

## Play hard

Three little kids run around the parking lot of the flea market without a care in the world. After a few moments of frolicking, they hear the commander's unique whistle signaling the kids it's time to start the day!

Cherokee looks at Wizzard, Wizzard looks at Yazzing, Yazzing looks at Cherokee, and with an unspoken agreement race to the entrance door of the flea market. Cherokee wanted to break-in her brand new NEW BALANCES. Wiz was just competitive, he would race barefoot, if it gave him the advantage. Yaz just wanted to have fun chasing his big brother. After catching their breaths, they silently glance at each other to qualify the winner of the post-dawn Saturday morning competition.

Noticing the exertion of each child's recreation, Popp glances towards the refreshments left on the end of the 6-foot sheeted table. Cherokee only took two gulps out of her 10 oz. orange juice before they went out to play. She guzzled down the other $\frac{5}{8}$ and used her short sleeve to wipe her mouth. Wizzard finished the half jug that left his lips light blue. He turned the jug upside down to drain the last drop. Yazzing, at 4 years old, was already showing his conservative side as he patiently sipped on his yellow, wannabe pineapple juice. He still had half left and showed no signs of finishing before the workday was to begin; and the earliest customers were about to enter the doors.

Popp looked at the kids with a commanding stare, and intentionally made the throat-clearing sound. Each child from various positions around the stall turned attentively to await the nod to start the family creed.

Popp nodded his head slightly after gazing into each child's psyche, and with the harmony of a church choir they each recited, *"We work hard for our bread and meat; if we don't work, we don't eat."*

Like a maestro waving his wand, the patriarch made a gesture with his hand, and this commenced the work day as the customers slowly started trickling in. Three of the competitive children selfishly targeted each prospect. Their tutelage was to tout the company's well drafted one-liner, *"Excuse me, do you have a favorite fragrance?"*, then simultaneously present a sample of one of the 300 most popular fragrances of that season.

These children knew the business well. After all, they had plenty of motivation to learn and master the techniques of a huckster. Popp was quite serious about teaching his youngest daughter and two grandsons the real elements of work and its rewards. Each child had to procure a sale before they could take the proceeds of that sale and go to the food court and buy the breakfast of their choice.

Wolf was 10 and had already mastered the craft of managing the family's oil stand. He was taught, once a prospect answered the catchphrase, he could segue them into a similar fragrance based on that favorite fragrance's top-note. He was a true artist to behold. As he applied the suggested fragrance inside the wrist on the pulse point, he would explain to the customer that the oil activated at 63°. Then he would expound, **"This is the reason salesmen prompt individuals to rub their wrists together."** While the client was rubbing their wrists to warm the oil and activate the fragrance, Wolf would reach for a second choice with the same top-note but a different bottom note.

Once he assured the prospect that the $7 bottle of oil had never been cut or adulterated, he would offer a deal of 2 for $10 as he was presenting the second fragrance. He was so skilled in this technique he was able to introduce 5 acceptable fragrances to which he would offer a deal of 5 for $20 and most of the time....would "GET it."

Wolf totally understood the $20 bill was the fastest way to $100 and many days he grossed $400 before the stall closed. He was irrefutably the 10-year-old Captain of <u>BNB essential oils & fragrances</u>.

This day, no one rested on their laurels. Everyone had to compete to eat. No exceptions!! Popp was touting, Wolf was touting and the two six-year-olds and the one four-year-old had to *"Work hard for their bread and meat; if they didn't work, they didn't eat!!"*

Like an Eagle, Popp was watching over the young brood; mainly to make sure they were using the proper approach to their prospects, and pronouncing the "catchphrase" loud enough and clear enough to affect an interaction.

Cherokee had developed a direct approach to literally stand in front of the prospect's walking path and peer two feet above her own eyes into her future clients eyes and proudly proclaim her pedigree as a salesperson- in-training and solicit, *"Excuse me, may I ask your favorite fragrance?"* Customer after endless customer would smile and congratulate a six-year old's professional and polite expertise that trademarked her family's entrepreneurship. A firm 60% of her attempts were rewarded with a 5-minute visit to her base of operations which was 2 six-foot tables connected end to end and filled with aromatherapy products. If they weren't enchanted, they would at least give a smile of support, or a congratulatory comment, which would definitely serve as encouragement to a child motivated to hone their craft. Some customers, content that they had completed their primary shopping, would re-visit the stand and seek out Cherokee to rekindle the spark she initiated. Others, once they completed their intended shopping, would bypass her with an additional congratulatory nod as they exited the market.

After Cherokee ushered Mrs. Henson over to the table, Wiz was inspired by the hope of engaging his own customer. He enthusiastically jerked on the sportcoat of the businessman rushing past the table. Oblivious to the 3 footer to his right, he looked down as if he snagged his jacket on the edge of the table.

Upon acknowledgment of the future salesman, the gent smiled a vote of respect, despite being 6 feet away by the time his eyes made contact. He made a hand gesture indicating he would stop by on his way back.

Wiz seemed to realize it would be more advantageous to solicit a prospect that wasn't moving so swiftly. He was able to test his theory on the young wanderer browsing over at Wally's cosmetic table. When the guy looked over his right shoulder to capture the various oddities abundant in a flea market, Wiz struck like a Cobra; *"Excuse me, can I ask you, what is your favorite perfume?"*

Popp smiled. Not quite the script he drafted but acceptable none the least.

The kind collegiate was instrumental in offering encouragement as well as guidance when he gently instructed, "I don't wear perfume but my favorite cologne is COOL WATER." Wiz was quite entertaining when he gestured "right this way" as he assured *We have that one, but it's body oil!! which lasts longer and costs less!"*

Popp was silently gleaming with pride as he pretended to be focused elsewhere.

Mr. Jones was magically intrigued as he seemed to be invisibly tethered to the soliciting hand gesture towards the oil stand. Obliging the young entrepreneur, the collegiate seemed star-struck to engage in this Wizzard's summons. He leaned forward to hear the artistry bellowing forth from this deep-voiced, miniaturized salesman.

*" COOL WATER you said?'*, as he reached for the bottle with the sky blue compound. "Excuse me Popp," slightly dismissing his grandfather with a brush of his left elbow, as if to imply, *'You're impeding my progress.'*

The collegiate with his blue and orange, MORGAN sweatshirt couldn't stop grinning as he extended his right upturned wrist. He initially began to extend his left, until he realized his CITIZEN watch would ruin the demonstration.

Wiz rolled the upturned ESSENCE counterclockwise in about seven small circles before he demonstrated how to rub the wrists together to activate the scent. He may have applied two circles too many but he wanted to ensure the rollerball hadn't gotten stuck, nor did he want to under-apply the first time. The fragrance had already started aerosolizing before the gent started rubbing his wrist, but this gave Wiz the seconds he needed to reach for the ACQUA DI DIO.

Wiz studied the man's facial expression as he loosened the top of his second fragrance. "Wow!, this is really good." the young man expressed as his face changed from being surprised by the unexpected quality of the product. His eyes scanned the titles of the other fragrances, neatly merchandised on the rack of 300 names.

*"Have you ever tried ACQUA DI GIO?"* Shocking the guy that he was, two steps ahead of him. "NO!" as he sniffed his right wrist again. His eyes closed slightly in disbelief of the exactitude and potency of this product. He eagerly slid his flex-band up the broader part of his left arm to reveal another pulse-point.

Wiz had already rolled the little ball to ensure it wasn't stuck before he moderately applied four circles of fragrance. Just when the fella was about to raise his arm, WIZ shouted "Hold up," while he reached over the oil diffuser display to grab the silver-plated chalice containing the coffee beans. *"Smell this!",* he advised, *"It will clear your nose',* he exhorted.

Overwhelmed with pride and joy, he obliged to the advice of the best sales experience he never imagined by a six-year-old.

Gauging his client's face, Wiz suggested, *"These uncut oils are $7 apiece, but I can give YOU... 2 for $10,... if you like!!*

The Morganite nodded in agreement while reaching for his wallet. Wiz slipped a business card in the 2 ½" x 4" plastic, zip lock bag. He demonstrated his tutelage by giving each bottle an extra tightening twist before inserting it into the cellophane with the labels aligned and facing outward and legible. He applied pressure to the zip lock and flipped the package over to ensure the business card was legible.

He received his $10, did his ceremonial *"Thank you and God Bless you!!"* Then looked over to the other six-foot table to see if Cherokee was finished with Mrs. Henson.

Wiz was satisfied with his first sale of the day, but impressed to see his aunt had a standard white plastic bag awaiting additional items. He could see the opaque image of a business card turned outward and pressed up against the surface of the bag by a 6"x5"x5" box. He knew by the imprint, Cherokee sold an oil diffuser and was probably in the process of suggesting a burning oil. He watched her do the extra twist on a 4oz bottle of ARABIAN SANDALWOOD and knew she was in for a big payday, and it wasn't even 8 a.m.

Cherokee, being Popp's youngest child as well as youngest business partner, at 6 years old, already had two years of experience over her nephews. Popp noticed from his oldest child to his youngest, at 4 years old they demonstrated intelligence and aptitudes which gave them abilities to comprehend entrepreneurial concepts.

One of his methods taught them the importance of customer service! Once the sale was completed and the merchandise was in the bag, the four-year-olds job was to place a business card in the bag, print side facing outward, tie the bag in bunny ears, present the completed sales with outstretched arms with one thumb in each opening and conclude the transaction by looking the customer in the eye while humbly, sincerely, and with a clear pronunciation, say, *"Thank you and God bless you"*.

Cherokee had the protocol down to a science, so Wiz knew it was time to go eat when he heard Cherokee conclude the transaction with Mrs. Henson.

Cherokee's routine was so polished it almost seemed as if she was performing a curtsey when she extended the package and slightly bowed her head.

They both looked to see what Yazzing was doing before they raced to the food court. He was still sippin' on his pineapple drink almost in bewilderment of what the others were doing. He initiated some tears when the Sixers were about to leave and Popp scolded, " Not you!!" Well not a harsh scold, but a lovingly, gentle, "scold". Yazzing was about to get a reality check of exactly what it meant, " *We work hard for our bread and meat; if we don't work we don't eat.* The reality check was sure to be exacerbated when Wizard returns with the savory fragrance of his favorite sausage, egg, and cheese on Mrs. Mary's homemade crescent roll.

Cherokee's chicken tamale added insult to injury with its grilled onions and roasted tomatoes. "Delightful" was her description when she closed her eyes and "Mmmmmed" an expression of gratitude. Yazzing's eyes teared even more, as his teammates teased him with their appetizing delights. Popp didn't try to console him, rather he tried to use the kids as motivation to encourage

11

Yazzing that he was equally capable to look an adult in the eye and clearly pronounce the catchphrase.

Popp even pointed to a browser that he thought might be susceptible to a child's solicitation. "See that lady with the pink skirt and white blouse? When she gets up here, ask her. "Excuse me, what's your favorite fragrance?" Yazzing looked as if he didn't hear a word he said. Noticing this, Popp assured Yazzing that if he didn't try he would not get anything to eat. This enacted another wave of tears and the lady was getting closer. Popp wiped his eyes and exhorted "You can do this, here she comes.!"

Yazzing looked in Popps eyes with all the trust in his soul. He sniffed up some boogers, and his grandfather pulled a Dunkin Donuts napkin from his pocket, he smelled it to make sure he hadn't used it to wipe any perfumes and put it to Yazzing's nose and told him to blow. The lady was three tables away so Popp urged Yazzing to lift his head so he could see if he had any more boogers. He always made Yazz laugh when he blew a surprising gust of air in his unsuspecting nostrils. This time was no different. His countenance changed and Popp used the opportunity to encourage him again. "You can do this, then you can go get anything you want to eat." This caused a great big smile and a ton of confidence.

" Excuse me, uhh, uh, like to smell my oils?", he stumbled." "Well sure!" she encouraged, as she ran her fingers through his curly hair." Right this way" as he emulated his big brother with a wave towards the table. "These are all oils not perfumes" he mimicked in his own interpretation. "That means they're better but they're cheaper though" he parroted, as best he could. "Hey Popp, come help Miss um um…. 'What's your name?" "Kay", she bluffed, as she obliged with any ole fake moniker it seemed. "Popp, help Miss Kay with her favorite perfume," he announced with his newfound confidence as he looked around to see how far the other kids had advanced in their breakfast.

He exuded a sense of accomplishment knowing he'd done his part to get the prospect to the table. There was no doubt he was about to eat his fave; bacon (fried hard), egg, and cheese, on Mrs. Mary's homemade crescent roll. He seemed to salivate with certainty, while unconsciously licking his lips. He was so sure Popp would close the deal, he physically turned away from the transaction, until Popp beckoned, "These are body oils not perfumes that's why they last longer, but cost less. Popp was a stickler for verbatim as well as continuity in advertising, so he reiterated key phrases to the kids to polish their techniques to the craft. Popp motioned to Yaz to watch and pay attention as he started the spiel from the beginning." Miss Kay," he pronounced, with clarity and professionalism," do you have a favorite fragrance?" He waited patiently for her to explore her mental library, while reaching for his staple,- **African Musk**- which was a 90% favorite amongst unisex fragrances. "Nahh, I can't say that I have a favorite. I like to try new things," she suggested in an innuendo. Popp acknowledged the innuendo but bypassed it in favor of closing the deal and teaching Yazz the process. However, he did display some subtle

13

sensuality when he gently turned her right wrist upward and used the hairy part of his right index finger to stroke the area where he was about to apply the oil. As Yazz was paying close attention, he changed the gesture to a warming circular motion with the side of his right palm while instructing Yaz, "this warms the pulse point to 63° to help the oil blend with the body's natural chemistry." Kay was impressed and attracted to Popp's savoir-faire, subtlety, and wisdom to instruct a four-year-old in the art of mastering a lifelong skill. She was so intrigued, she briefly fantasized the older gentleman as husband material.

With the pulse-point warmed and all parties attuned to the process, Popp applied 4 circular counterclockwise applications of body oil to Kay's inner wrist. To add to his sex appeal, he blew a smooth, steady stream of warm air into Kay's wrist, trusting that Yazz, at 4 years old, would have assumed the play was innocent and part of the obvious warming process. Respectively, trusting that Kay would accept his gesture as a response to her innuendo. Kay, delicately eased her arm away from Popp's suave captivation, while peering in his eyes, in anticipation of something sweeping her off her feet; either Popp or the aroma.

"Mmmmm," she murmured, in sultry acceptance, "what isss this???" she elongated, as her suggestive eyes questioned! "African Musk " he boldly proclaimed, taking full responsibility for the double entendre. "I'll take it," maintaining her magnetism, while inquiring, "do you have more?" Yazz tuned

14

back in from his fantasy when he heard, "I'll take it!!" He had zero interest in the courting rituals; only ideas of delicacies and choices.

Popp, on the other hand, was wondering if Kay liked fingers in her curly hair. "There's plenty more where that came from," he clichéd. "I'm interested," she affirmed.

In a snapback of reality, she quipped, "how much are these things??" He maintained his Playbook when answering, "these uncut body oils are $7, but I...can give YOU...two for $10." He was fine with the courting, but not so much as to forget making the sale. "Do you take checks?" she joked. But he was not joking when he boasted, "we take cash, checks, money orders, and credit cards!" as he lifted the antenna on the portable credit card machine, hidden snuggly behind the steps of the oil rack. "Oh WOWWW!!" she exclaimed, "give me another one to add to the African musk, make the other, light, citrusy, and floral" she hastened, reaching for her wallet.

Popp wanted to dazzle her with his expertise. He chose **Issey Miyake** to guarantee a steady stream of compliments from her audience. She was equally grateful for the contrast of aromas. They both expressed different aspects of Kay's personality. Popp allowed Yazz to close the deal with the protocol of placing the business card outward in the ziplock; giving the bottles (fresh bottles not the sample bottles used for the demonstration) an extra tightening, placing the labels outward- legibly, extending his arms and blessing the family's customers with"Thank you and God bless you!!" Kay was turned on

15

even more, seeing how pop included manners, gratitude, and most importantly, **GOD,** in his tutelage.

She ended her interaction with, "I'll call you later for more!"
She looked twice as sexy leaving, as she did coming!

Popp showed Yazz the credit card receipt. He wanted to introduce him to the eternal world of numbers, date's, and times, as well as the $10 sale he procured. He also wanted to emphasize an impact on the electronic form of money as he reached in his pocket and pulled out 10- $1 bills to use as counting tools for his grandson.

The flea market was starting to fill and Popp could no longer have a line of sight to see his children amongst the crowd. He asked Wally to keep an eye on Wolf as he signaled for the other kids to join him while he gave purchasing and change counting lessons to Yazzing.

Wolf made three sales while they were gone. He assured Popp that the first sale was only $7 and that's his portion of the $27 to eat with. Popp was proud of his son's integrity and relieved him to go get breakfast.

Sales were moderate that Saturday but Popp took advantage of every teachable moment, after all he only had these opportunities on the weekend.

It was only 2:30 pm on this Saturday's summer afternoon. There was still plenty of sunlight left after the stall was closed. The car was packed and the kids were ready for some weekend fun.

While checking to ensure every child was wearing a seatbelt, Popp asked, " What do you guys want to do now?" Wolf suggested, "Go driving." Cherokee dittoed, "Yeah!" Wiz was undecided, and Yazzing said, " Ride the trains." He was referring to the Metrorail at Union Station with it's different colored Rail lines which made the subway map quite interesting to Yazzing.

One time Popp made up an interesting teaching game; where he plotted 4 different colleges, located in 4 different colored rail lines, assigned each child a college corresponding to a specific color, then showed them on the map where they were at Union Station, and challenged them to find the course of their chosen College. Yazzing was the first to find his college on the blue line which sparked lots of praise and admiration from Popp as well as the others.

The patriarch decided since the empty industrial parking lot was two miles from the flea market they would go there for Wolf's driving lessons then try to make it to Union Station.

There was no way to tell if Renee prepared dinner for the kids since he hadn't checked in yet. He knew there was plenty of food at Union Station, but it would total $50 in expenses once the fares were added.

When Popp pulled into the gas station, Wiz blurted out "MOTOCROSS!!" Everyone burst out laughing at his lateness. Even Yaz

17

smirked at his brother's delay. As they pulled into the industrial park, Wolf's face contorted with glee and expectation. He had begun to loosen his restraints in anticipation of getting behind the wheel. He was the closest to the front passenger door and he was the only one who had to get out. After he got out, he looked back to be sure that Cherokee wasn't following him, then slammed the heavy off-track door of the 1982 Mercury Marquis. He did some kind of Cossack leg kick, then reached to the sky like he was putting on a sport coat that was too tight. He shrugged his shoulders and grinned all the way around the back of the car. They all laughed at his excited goofy gestures as Popp just shook his head while sliding across the long bench seat.

Wolf got in and cracked his interlocking fingers by turning his palms outwards and extending his arms. He grinned at Popp with a half- certain, half-uncertain smirk; suggesting that he knew the procedures of: adjusting the seat, buckling up, adjusting mirrors, etc. He went through the steps and looked to Popp for assurance that he didn't forget anything. The excited lad reached for the key in the ignition and looked at Popp again. With no reaction from his teacher, he cranked the engine. He checked the mirrors again, put the lever in drive, and started on his imaginary course over the huge parking lot.

Popp was quiet, as he gave his son autonomy and liberty to evolve through this rite of passage.

Wiz, on the other hand, was not quiet. He unleashed from his seatbelt, and leaned forward over the back seat with arms folded, and was quite intrigued with his uncle having leisure to do what all young boys wish to do - DRIVE!! He earnestly and passionately with Christmas-like expectation asked, "Can I go next?" Popp didn't hesitate to say "Sure" since he was wondering if any of the other kids desired to feel the wheel. In addition to granting Wiz his desires, he tested the other two with a quick survey, ``Who wants to go after Wiz?" Like a student in class, Cherokee raised her hand, but like a Hitler salute, so Popp could acknowledge through his periphery. Yaz was a tad bit late, when he softly said, "Me Popp, I want to go after Wiz." Although Wiz initiated the extracurricular recreation, Popp had several different protocols he liked to teach the children to prepare them for real-life. One- was the practice, "the last shall be the first; another, he would line up by age, either ascending or descending.

Wolf was literally already in the driver's seat. If Popp chose a descending order it would make Cherokee next. She was three days older than her nephew. Popp settled the matter by explaining to Wiz that he was gonna let his aunt go next since she was already on the front seat and all she had to do was climb over once Wolf got out. Wiz retorted, "All I gotta do is climb over too!" Popp loved his kids to be able to banter, as well as speak up for themselves; however, this was bordering on mutiny. Grandfather agreed with his first grandchild for making a good point but explained he was using the unfair-age-system. Wiz was unmoved, especially since he felt entitled by the mere suggestion. He dropped down into the deep back seat, pouting and

19

mumbling, "What...ever!" arms folded and all. Yaz was patient, in his satisfaction of opportunity, as he looked at his brother in disbelief for his ingratitude and insolence. Cherokee appeared to be expressionless, while her countenance was jumping for joy with anticipation and excitement. Popp was too observant of how smoothly Wolf was handling the big boxed car to attend to Wiz's insubordination, he was sly and cunning, and would be sure to make him apologize when his turn came to drive. Fifteen minutes of intensity seemed as long as a rollercoaster ride to Wolf as he neatly parked the vehicle in the same spot from where he started.

Cherokee was unbuckled and climbing across her dad before Wolf even put the lever in park. Knowing she could neither see over the dashboard nor reach the pedal, Popp paused from giving her directions to witness her analytical skills. She proved she had been listening when she reached to put on the seatbelts. Then the epiphany, when she sat buckled with a blank expression because she hadn't figured the next step. Wolf entered and sat in the vacant seat. Popp was still enjoying Cherokee's bewilderment, then asked, "Would you like to sit on my lap and steer? I'll control the brake and acceleration and you can control the wheel?" he suggested.

Without hesitation, she loosened the straps, excited to have any solution other than "You can't drive then." She climbed through the restraints and Popp slid over. He still went through the protocol of adjusting mirrors and all before he allowed her to crank the ignition. The first crank didn't ignite. Most likely she was afraid for whatever reason. She looked to her father for his usual wisdom to life's challenges but he was mute, usually suggesting "Try it again." She yielded to the silent advice and turned over the big engine. Wiz popped out of his obstinacy and jumped back to his post on the back of the seat; vicariously delighting in his aunt's opportunity. He certainly had to be anticipating that he was on deck.

The teacher released the brake but didn't accelerate. The idling and the gradual momentum was more than enough speed within the huge lot for a six-year-old. She began to seesaw the steering wheel the way children do when they pretend to drive but this was real life and the large boat was rocking to her every whim. Before Popp could suggest that she follow the white lines, she gave the steering wheel a quick 90° snap to the left. Dad instinctively smashed the brake and everything and everyone inside the vehicle hurled.

Yazzing was the only one still strapped in. His reaction indicated it was merely a sudden stop, although that didn't explain why his brother was suddenly in his lap. Wolf's reflexes obviously had him to brace himself with the dashboard. Popp's reflexes grabbed an empty steering wheel and they all burst out in laughter when a voice from the passenger side floor blurted, "Oh yeah, ..seat belts!"

Wiz must have developed some acuity from the video games he couldn't stay away from, because he actually seemed to have a handle (Excuse the Pun!) on this driving business. He even asked Popp to speed up a little. His

21

grand-pop obliged, and he maintained a reasonable amount of control with each increase. Of course, the insatiable one wasn't satisfied with his 15-minute drive, but he'd get over it.

Next up was the patient, almost oblivious...Yazzing! Calmly sitting atop his mentor's lap listening to the driving protocols, he looked straight ahead presumably mapping his intended course because this 4-year-old drove that big bodied Gran Marquis with the fluidity of an airline pilot. He was so gentle and accurate in his autonomous 90° turns, that he would make a testing officer proud. He certainly surprised and made his grandfather proud, that he got his time extended beyond 15 minutes. He remained humble with all the accolades and only wanted to climb over the back seat like his big brother did when he was finished.

They all boasted about how well they did and of course shared their opinions and some criticism on how each other drove. Yaz, as nonchalant as he was about the criticism, actually did the most outstanding job, considering he was only 4 years old.

Popp stayed quiet until Renee called. Ahhh...! "Answer the phone one of y'all", he interrupted. "Hello", Wolf said in his mature voice. "Hold on please," displaying manners. "Yeah hon" in the silence, 'on our way to Union Station." "You did?", was next, "Okay, about 20 minutes." He hung up. "Renee wants us to come home, dinner is ready. "What's she making?" Wiz encroached. "I didn't ask, but I'm getting hungry," Popp replied. "Me too, "both sets of siblings harmonized with each other.

At Popp's, Renee took charge once the crew returned. "Y'all wash your hands," she bellowed, "Cherokee, you sit over here next to me. I need to explain these receipts and show you how I do the accounting and the deposit slips for these checks." "Y'all boys won't have long before the sun goes down, so I suggest you enjoy some time out in the yard. If you play in the backyard, watch the poop, your grandfather didn't clean it up," she shaded.

"Yazzing is first in the tub tonight, the rest of y'all know the routine from there," she continued instructing.

Popp eased his plate away from the dictator's purview and retreated to his recliner in the basement with his cold brew.

He and Renee were oblivious to the fight Wiz got into with the kids from another block, and no one was gonna tell how Wiz wrestled the 9-year-old down to the ground, put his hands around his neck and grimacingly swore that he would kill him.

The dirt on his knees didn't give it away either, both adults assumed it to be the casualty of male bonding.

They had an encouraging morning, an enlightening afternoon, an eventful evening and the night ended with Wolf popping Wizzard upside the head for trying to dominate the remote.

.40 Cal:  "Her nephew was killed with one; and she didn't like it !!

# 2nd Quarter

## Work Harder

## Play Harder

A lot has happened in 5 years. Not only did Popp and the kid's mom divorce; he and Renee were no longer together.

Wiz and Yazzing's mom had 3 more kids, and the youngest was an infant.

Wolf fared well in the School for the Arts. He was extremely proud to be attending the same school that his cousins {Anthony Leonard-owner of SOUTHERN BLUES}; his cousin {KEDRIC GOUGH owner of GEORGIA PEACH}; TUPAC and {JADA PINKETT SMITH- local mega-actress, and Hollywood mogul} attended.

A guidance counselor from his middle school noticed his artistic ability. He vouched for him, and suggested he seek additional education there.

After the divorce, he lost some of his focus on his school work. It seemed to manifest in his doodling. His drawings were not macabre, red and black expressions of doom. Nor were they the fragmented distortion of a schizo - Picasso era. Nevertheless, they exuded some kind of expression.

He drew pictures of the entire family. A lot of them had a boy on a dirt bike. There were no drawings of matricide or patricide, however, he did punch his father in the jaw when he was informed in the family meeting that the parents were dissolving. There were depictions of a boy playing football - ALONE! A lot of it was artistic expansions of his name, maybe he was contemplating becoming a tattoo artist or maybe he was thinking of his name in lights. Whatever it was, it attracted the attention of his middle school teacher; who not only liked it, he endorsed a scholarship to get him into the prestigious academy.

The first year in the BSA was totally devoted to visual arts. By the second year, another teacher from the academy recognized a musical talent and catapulted him into the musical sphere of wind instruments. It was recognized that he could play any wind instrument he put his mind to, so another wise - GODSENT - suggested he try the variety of the FRENCH HORN. Not only did it work out, it earned him another scholarship.

Emotionally, the divorced-teen years proved to be challenging. He continued to work, but not with as much enthusiasm. He actually inherited the oil stand, and became the only 15 year old vendor who owned his business at the flea market, but with his mom infuriated with his dad for allowing Renee to manipulate a divorce, she deliberately and defiantly refused to take him to the flea market. He was a great driver by then, yet still too young to be licensed.

The offspring lived 30 minutes north of the flea market. Popp lived 30 minutes south. With the children becoming pawns in a custodial chess game, the weekend commutes became a whole new production of sorts.

The emotional and custodial despair transcended into professional despair, and before long, Popp divorced the business also.

Things started looking up for Wolf after he got his first piece of pussy from a cute, petite theatrical student. His great fortune happened behind the curtains of the stage. That 'curtainly' put some pep back in his step!

*

Cherokee too had misgivings about her dad and the divorce.
Not only was she holding a grudge about his choice of discipline regarding an incident at the flea market a few years ago, she felt subconsciously she was the cause of the divorce.

A few years ago, the nephews didn't come down for the weekend to spend with Cherokee and Wolf at Popp and Renee's. Being a 7 year old at the flea market wasn't as much fun for her without the other children her age in the crowded land of giants. She was beginning to show signs of boredom, discontent and rebellion. Business was extremely good that day and Popp and Wolf were fortunately very busy and too engaged to responsibly keep eyes on a bored and defiant Pisces. Several direct commands were scoffed at and disregarded by her at a time when predators were on the rise in that area.

As a matter of fact, an unassuming, handsome, personable, 30ish, Latin guy had been regularly coming by the stand making purchases and striking up great topics of communication that he and Popp would indulge in for hours. One day, Julio came by with a beautiful teenage girl just around Wolf's age. Although Julio was vivacious and jubilant in his presentation to invite the kids on some child retreat for the weekend, his prop appeared distraught, dejected, and enslaved in her subdued role as his daughter who was supposed to have so much fun at this so-called child's camp.

When Popp decided this was the exact teachable moment to inform his daughter of the wiles and illusions of the real world, he called her to come out back to have a private - DADDY/DAUGHTER talk- about snakes in the garden.

When he summoned her to follow him to the meeting, she folded her arms, and defiantly slowed her pace. In the extremely crowded aisle, the slowed pace put her behind Popp-2:1 paces, and rushing shoppers were passing between their line of sight. Popp walked back towards her recalcitrance; when he reached her, he leaned forward and commanded through his clenched teeth, "come on Cherokee, this is not the time nor place for this." She grunted another layer of rebellion. Popp walked back again and put his hand behind the nape of her neck and sped her pace out the back door where the vendor vehicles were parked. When he was sure she was out of range from being hit by someone coming out of the door, he faced her to begin his speech.

She still had her arms folded when he introduced his untimely lecture with, "I'm telling you this because I love you." At that moment she shrugged her shoulders defiantly as if to contend "That's bullshit." His reflex popped her atop her braided crown while she was simultaneously ducking and turning away from the swing. His secondary reflex landed a controlled boot to her hind parts. The dual momentum propelled her to topple over head first towards the ground.

When she recovered, her posture and attitude resumed to the obedient child he was familiar with. With a contrite and receptive demeanor, he was able to inform her of the attempt made by a charismatic stranger, to not only dupe her, but to make the ultimate target of the ruse - the parent.

Although she returned to normal behavior and appeared to move past that teachable moment, something definitely changed in their bond, especially since she certainly perceived the encounter to be child abuse.

The other burden this young child subconsciously carried was the cross that she was responsible for the parent's divorce.

"What had happened was!" When Cherokee was 4 years old, she innocently, and honestly blurted out her and her mom ROCHELLE'S whereabouts when Popp asked, "What took y'all so long to get home?" The baby blurted out, "Mommy was kissing Mr. Donnie!" Popp reflexed, in front of the child, by doing a judo flip on Rochelle and laying her on the floor when he realized -midway-what had occurred. The witnessing child screamed and ran to her mom's aid, issuing a side glance of disgust towards her reactive father. That was another incident the burdened child had to undergo without therapy during the aftermath of the family divorce.

The incident caused Rochelle to enforce an edict. "Tell absolutely-no one-our personal family business." An edict which got carried out and enforced throughout the child's rearing.

She's 11 now and seems to be adjusting to the changes that the divorce created. They still go with Popp occasionally on the weekend, but not at Mrs. Renee's, now it's Miss Liza's. She misses her camaraderie with her same-age nephews, but she still gets to drive. She enjoys gymnastics, modern dance, and track at the local recreation center after school during the week. She's developed awesome habits of study and discipline and has vowed to become a lawyer. She's bonded with many more cousins her age, on her mom's side, and is well respected by all.

*

Popp expanded his business, maybe too far! Miss Renee envied the supplemental income being made on the weekend at the flea market; which allowed Popp to use the proceeds to pay his portion of the joint bills without encroaching on his income from the job where they met.

In addition to being a driver for the governmental contractor at WOLTERS KLUWER, he was a PFA (personal financial analyst) at PRIMERICA. This enabled him the skills and resources to analyze her expenditures versus income, and make recommendations on how to close the gap.

Once he discovered the $600 being spent on fast food each month, he implemented a monthly meal plan for her based on the delights she enjoyed for breakfast, lunch, and dinner. He showed her that by taking the time to extrapolate her desires for lunch, she could cook her favorite meals on Sunday and use leftovers for lunch throughout the week. He anticipated the monetary effect and extrapolated tertiary meals to make the experiment fun and achievable. He even considered her favorite snack when they went shopping once a month to acquire the goods for the plan.

His half of the bills were being made at the flea market in one day. If you factor in the investments and profits, he'd definitely clear his portion in two weekends.

She wanted the same financial freedom. So he set her up a duplicate stand in the far side of town. She was to run that branch and regardless of the profits, use the collective revenue to offset the portion of her bills.

She was a faithful, on-time, and dedicated vendor. However, she was totally devoid of the enthusiasm needed to stop-attract-and procure the sales that would translate into a booming business.

Popp also branched out into the prestigiously eclectic venue in D.C. The vendor next to him was selling antiques. The vendor across from him was selling vintage furs. Both businesses were booming! He quickly realized he had to adapt a strategy to attract his share of clientele to his aromatherapy franchise.

He analyzed that he was seemingly invisible to the regular passersby. Next, he reversed engineered a scenario where he was the customer and questioned what would attract his attention if he was gawking at vintage items. What he concluded seemed to be a stroke of genius.

First, he deduced he needed to appeal to the oldest tracking device known to animals - the OLFACTORY system. There is a profound reason the NOSE is foremost in the grand design of the face. He needed to have the scents of the most acceptable fragrances cascading across the venue. Next, to compete with the touts of the charismatic BAJAN, he needed to reverse engineer a catchphrase. He imagined himself being drawn by his eyes delight to an antique or a vintage fur and asked himself what other senses could compete with visual attraction. He deduced the nose, then solved that problem; but for the ears,he needed a catchphrase to convince shoppers they may be ignoring the most feasible value of the day. He rearranged the concept to be a one-liner but it was a long one-liner. It needed to maintain the integrity of the catchiness, with the brevity of a tout-phrase. The shortest he was able to get it down to was, "Excuse me, don't bypass the best deal in the flea market!" YEAH! He exclaimed in his creative mind. He couldn't wait to try it out.

The next day, as he was setting up to light the candle and vaporize the selection he'd chosen to attract customers, he noticed a fine, ALMOND-SKINNED, NUBIAN, NATURELLE about 10 tables down the main aisle. She had buns like SERENA WILLIAMS and breasts to match. Her long eyelashes were natural, and her sneakers weren't even tied. She had on a quality female version of a solid - colored BILL COSBY sweater, and a very Parisian scarf draped at her neck. She absolutely, positively, didn't notice his fragrance or the table at all, as she was bee-lining towards the furs. She was already purveying on the opposite side of the wide main aisle and at least 4 tables from her destination. His timing had to be as accurate as a hunter stalking a gazelle. He began the count down: 4 tables, 3 tables, 2 tables, and with a deep directed voice, "DON'T bypass...the best deal in **this** flea market!" her head turned, but her feet didn't.

There was some satisfaction that the catch-phrase worked, but perhaps it needed modifying or was it her personality that was disinterested.

He watched her continue on her westward stroll along the opposite side of the aisle. She turned right and went up that aisle, then down the long corridor of vendors.

The closer her orbit came to being within earshot; he thought he'd give one more modified attempt. "I noticed you didn't give THIS vendor ...5...of

33

your precious minutes." With a matter of fact, "OH YEAH!," she redirected her course, and headed straight for his venue. The very first thing she touched on the table, an indigo and crystal pyramid... dropped and broke...and it wasn't even for sale. It was for de'cor and a personal favorite. After the 'oopses," and "I'm sorries," and the discussion about its value and compensation, she became more contrite. It must've been her strong personality, because, even though-contrite-she still flipped his personal chair from behind the vendor line, faced him, sat down, and said, "you have 5 minutes...GO!!"

He asked her name. "LIZA", she said, dismissively, "Keep going!" He was shocked by her initial terseness, but he didn't show it. This compelled him to switch gears, and he expounded on the definition and origin of her name. From 10:30 am until 5:30 pm., she sat in that chair, and they conversed about everything from Aerodynamics to Zoo locations. She even threw her life story in there somewhere.

She helped him break down his stand, load his car, and even treated him to a Stromboli from the bistro on the corner. The running joke of the day was the double entendre of his catch-phrase.

She recalled several times throughout their interaction how she thought it was intriguing whether it was him or his merchandise that he was referring to as the "best deal in the flea market." They laughed each time she joked about it.

*

That wasn't the only expansion made.

The lady Miss Kay turned out to be Miss Kenya! She became a representative for BNB Oils! Her first purchase was a $1,500 order of racks and oils. She procured her very own venues that included flea markets, stores, and personal clientele.

They were sleeping together regularly. That is...until someone felt entitled to her cousin as well. However, he was psychoanalytically remorseful...of expanding his business toooo...far!

Later, the same Sunday he met Liza, it seemed rather ominous when he returned home, that Renee was nowhere to be found and wasn't answering her phone.

Popp was aware, her ex-Arnie had come home from prison. Despite numerous denials of being interested in his reappearance, Popp was convinced that she may have had a vested interest in his return. The town they lived in was quaint and most of Renee's family and activities were congealed in an area called OAK CREST. Oak Crest had a 2 block square park where the community got together to have cookouts.

There was ample daylight this day before the sun was to set. The park was two miles away and Popp viewed the ride as exercise. He wondered where he left his brass knuckles, then remembered he was a changed man; still changing, but nonetheless changed...and he promised everyone who loved him, he wouldn't be going back to prison either. He defeated his old mindset, at

.40 Cal: "Her nephew was killed with one; and she didn't like it !!

least that portion of it, in lieu of letting the two know his ole-STREET-Spidey senses were still intact.

When he straddled his bike, before he placed his foot on the pedal, he looked up to the crisp blue sky and fluffy white clouds and inhaled the air of freedom. He remembered a few things he prayed about while he was incarcerated and was proud he didn't seek any weapons to carry on this adventure. Next...he said a faithful prayer, thanking GOD for removing the intent to harm despite his violently abusive modeling.

With that, he ventured out to exercise, enjoying the blue skies, and fluffy clouds along the way. The prayer must've manifested a stealthy, non-verbal approach. He noticed the back of her canary ruffled, sleeveless blouse. He rode across the grass on his mountain bike, directly down the blindspot of her spine. When her suitor's eyes indicated someone was directly behind her, she turned around. The instant she made eye contact and acknowledgement, he turned around and rode off into the sunset. His bike was out of the grass and steady on the street, and the last she saw of him was a silhouette when he dropped his hands and balanced freestyle into the setting sun.

He went home, threw his stuff in some bags, and booked a week stay in the motel around the corner. He left the bike. Perhaps, he thought, her teenage son could use it.

He'd blocked all Renee's calls and within a week, he had communicated with Liza often.

She was super eager to show him her recently purchased new home in the nearby county. The tour was extensive. She showed the bathroom, the basement, including the closets. Unbeknownst to Liza, Popp's eidetic memory recorded several articles of clothing hanging there...men's clothes. He captured shoe sizes, arm lengths, jackets, and hats.

Luckily, he did; next weekend he's working alone. A stranger appears asking irrelevant questions about the "Peppermint Sensation"; one of the inventor's 18 inventions using the Kosher essence Yakima Peppermint. The thing is...Popp sells the ESSENCE of peppermint to select customers in his Essential Oil division of BNB Oils.

A couple of things made him extremely suspicious: 1) he didn't resonate with the statement, "Tell me about this peppermint." 2) he had on a blue trench coat, a hat with a Fibonacci spiral in front and a pair of tan Hush Puppies...all articles he saw in Liza's vestibule closet during the tour. Well not the tan Hush Puppies, they were in something like the guest room.

Popp knew to study this sucker's features thoroughly. Once he was sure the character left the premises, he decided to do a little phishing of his own.

He called Liza and put several things to the test. First, he let her know he saw men's shoes in the guest room and asked if she rented to boarders, suggesting that he didn't intend to continue paying the motel prices in his transition.

.40 Cal: "Her nephew was killed with one; and she didn't like it !!

Fortunately, she was honest in divulging that she came to the state with her estranged husband.   He worked for AMTRAK and traveled a lot.  The relationship dissolved but their agreement allowed him a place to stay when he was in town and she didn't give a damn where he stayed when he was out of town.  In addition to the residence, he was allowed to use one of her cars.

When he told her what the stranger was wearing and what he said, she was able to deduce he must have listened to one of the landline phones in the basement because he had done it before.

Noting the time, but not disclosing his intent, Popp asked where 'dude' was most likely to be going.  She checked the time and said he must be on his way to his other job at the Marriott Hotel in nearby D.C.

He asked her to give him the dudes name and phone number so he could have a man to man talk with him.  He didn't mention, his style was vis-a-vis.

Informed with ample intel, he packed up and hurried to the hotel. The dude was miraculously entering the establishment when Popp noticed the one and only parking spot in D.C. available for the big-bodied vehicle. He viewed this as an omen. "God will deliver your enemy into your hands!"

Popp was named after St. (Saint) ANTHONY, but every so often the St. stands for *street* ANTHONY.  Right now, he was undoubtedly in St. (street) ANTHONY mode!

Being totally confident that the last person Jerry expected at his place of employment would be ST. (street) ANTHONY, he stealthily positioned himself behind the cover of the potted palm trees and dialed the number provided. He especially wanted to watch Jerry's response as he hurried across the huge lobby floor towards the double swinging doors that led to a kitchen department.

Again, the timing was impeccable. He asked Jerry when he answered the phone, "How long will it take for you to bring Liza's car and house key out to this lobby where the burnt orange carpet is with the olive green leather chairs?"

Jerry's neck pivoted so fast, it seemed like the phone was suspended in mid-air for a few milliseconds. That was a perfect moment for Street to push the "END" button on the call.

Street watched through the fronds of the palm bushes as Jerry searched high and low, east and west for a visual on the mystery caller! The prey was caught in the cross hairs of clocking in and searching for a ghost; the perfect position, as far as Street was concerned. Now, he waited!!

Might as well read the Wall Street Journal the hotel provided, he thought.

It was assumed to take at least 15 minutes before the phone was expected to ring. Jerry needed to clock in to secure his employment; call Liza to bitch about some stranger arriving unexpected at someone's place of employment. Find a co-worker willing to be his eyes and involve himself in his personal business and get his heart out at his throat to face the MAN who is about to evict him and repo the car.

Street turned the volume on his phone down to MUTE. He didn't want the ringtone to echo throughout the huge lobby and reveal his whereabouts the way Jerry's phone did when Street called it to make sure he spied the right guy.

Street got a kick out of popping the paper open and covering his face with it like the spies used to do in the old movies. He didn't mind being wrong in two of his calculations:

1) Just how long it would take for Jerry to appear in his work uniform.

2) Just how bad Liza would cuss his dumb ass out; because a few minutes later he exposed himself in the middle of the lobby with both sets of keys in his hands.

Street used a strategy, reminiscent of "the Art of War", namely, to attack your opponent in the most vulnerable place to force a surrender without casualty, loss, or waste of ammunition.

The place of employment acted as a leash to somewhat control explosive outburst. The time (the beginning of the shift) would aid in his decision making process as to whether or not he could afford a day of lost wages in view of being car-less and homeless. The middle of the open expanse served well to control his indignant response.

Street was polite and respectful when he asked, "What day will you be picking up your things?" However, he was rough and gruff when he snatched the keys from his hands. It probably was a subconscious response to Jerry's audacity to come to the flea market phishing.

As he was walking towards the door with the booty, he looked over his shoulder to the man still watching, and said, "Your stuff will be at the front door, if you don't come before this month ends, it WILL be on the front porch!!"

With that he exited and headed towards Liza's. Again he may have expanded too far, but...Oh shit...there is no but!!

Maybe he could self-soothe by convincing himself that his Zodiac sign is compelled by the expansive Jupiter or something, who knows?

He and Liza's 7 year relationship started shortly after the eviction. Guess who's driving the Honda Accord now???

*

Popp hadn't seen WIZ for quite some time. As soon as he leaned on the fence of the school ground and bellowed his signature whistle, a white-tooth sweaty spectacle came running towards him.

A welcomed sight to behold, the smile of his first grandchild brought absolute Divine worship into his soul. He adored this soul, no matter how misguided. Knowing his daughter was 15 years old during his conception, he placed no blame whatsoever on the child's misdirection.

.40 Cal: "Her nephew was killed with one; and she didn't like it !!

After exuberant salutations and reminiscent phrases, Wiz says, "Popp...watch this!!!" As Popp is intrigued watching Wiz bring his hands towards his mouth, he assumes his grandchild has practiced the signature whistle and is about to demonstrate, but the presentation takes a whole new meaning when a powerfully intended beckon comes through Wizard's parenthetically cupped hands, "HOO DEE HOOOOOO!!! HOO DEE HOOOO!!! HOO DEE HOOOOOO!!! Within a few seconds, 9..., I repeat...9 little soldiers came running from every direction towards the beckoning. Some...demonstrating more speed and loyalty than others, yet nonetheless, all responding to the bellow of their young gang leader.

Popp was shocked and amazed at what he was witnessing, that it brought up tears that didn't flow.

Tears crowded in the back of his throat as his grandson introduced, by pointing out three of the first responders, "This is my crew!!!"

The reformed grandfather couldn't believe his ears, but trusted his eyes, as the leader of his daughters' five children, transposed that skill into leading a 10 member crew of intelligent, loyal, and fearless gangsters at the age of 11.

With those ingredients, it certainly didn't take long before the band of comrades carved out a reputation, as well as a territory!

\*

.40 Cal: "Her nephew was killed with one; and she didn't like it !!

"SINISTER" is a word Popp never heard his daughter use, but that's exactly how she explained the expression on her oldest child's face when she told her father what was on the video the States attorney played in court two years later.

Unfortunately, two rival gangs were on the same bus. They were the CRUDS, the others were the BLIPS. Apparently Wizzard was rewarding a few of his key members for a great day of business by treating them to the mall for some grub and a movie.

The excited crew members who had never been to the County were piled in the back of the bus, joking around with hopes and high expectations of enjoying something they never had after "Working hard for their BREAD and MEAT."

As "URBAN PHENOMENA" would have it, two stops before their desired destination, four members of their rival group boarded the bus waving their ORANGE flags.

When the team in the front noticed the PURPLE bandanas in the back, the energy on the bus changed. The air was so eerily still; you could hear a cotton ball fall to the floor.

Wiz had his back turned; he was doing some of his signature comedic scripts when he felt the eeriness and noticed everyone's eyes were wide and beaming past his act.

.40 Cal: "Her nephew was killed with one; and she didn't like it !!

In the breadth between milliseconds, he even thought he noticed different scents of fear. He quickly scanned for glass to see the images behind him before he turned to face the problem. The only reflection available was the bus window displaying prominent images of 4 proudly worn bright Orange bandanas coming from the front of the bus.

Upon turning and eyeing his Arch-Rival from his Middle School, he dropped his defiantly lit cigar and smashed it into the floor of the bus with his fresh pair of Nike boots.

No immediate action took place from the initial recognition, but various huddles formed and there were whispers, murmurs and mumblings.

Knowing there were only two stops left. Wiz signaled to one of the crew to ring the bell.

Apparently, he contrived a plan already. As the bus slowed to the stop he gestured with a head shrug for the crew to exit from the back of the bus while he proclaimed his dominance by walking past the team of Blips and exiting at the front of the bus.

No doubt, there were eye frowns, mean mugs, and...oh yeah!...the subtle display of the butt of a .357 magnum as he walked past the gang and exited through the front door.

As the smaller team jeered, taunted and commented, Wizard maintained his composure while exiting as he surmised the head count and accounted for the last member leaving the rear of the bus. He quickly rushed back and grabbed the opened rear door and rushed in pulling his huge firearm from, who knows where?, and aimed into the crowd towards the front of the transit vehicle.

At least 2 of the Blips had 9mm's, and shots rang out in both directions. One of Wizzards stray bullets nearly missed the transit operator. The only passengers were the Blips, who took cover wherever they could inside the vehicle, while the Cruds scurried from the scene.

However the westsiders managed to make it out of the county, is a testament to how well trained they were in the skill of evasion.

Wiz mixed-matched the 9 outfits to make: One light-skinned Crud-end up in all black from head to toe; he had another match-up in red belt, red shirt, red sneakers, and blue jeans.

He separated 3 groups of 3 members. There were 3 brownskin team members that all had caps that he sent to the mall as diversions.. Another mixed-matched set took the guns and caught 3 different buses to the clubhouse in the city. He and 2 loyalists, in different clothes than the clothes captured in the transit video, spotted 2 bicycles in a county yard. One other bicycle provided joy to its grade school owner and Wiz directed Carrot to grab that bike, while he and Took boosted the easy marks.

The trio was very familiar with the biking trails through the woods.

The idea was for everyone to wait until the sun went down, change clothes again and meet at the alternate meeting place.

That night proved to be a successful evasion by gang standards, but the other team didn't seem to follow the gang-gang standards of not snitching. Despite the authorities having adequate video of the incident. The schoolmate provided as much personal information on Wiz as he could muster, even his government name, and names of family and friends.

Anyway, two years after Popp had seen his first grandchild in a long time, he was receiving news that the newly elected Mayor SHELLY DYSON was seeking juvenile life (13-18 year olds) sentences on Wizard for discharging a firearm within city limits, reckless endangerment and unlawful use of a firearm by a minor.

Popp was astounded as he propounded, meditated and prayed about, how much can happen in a span of 5-7 years!

Yazzing, on the other hand, as much as people thought they were twins, and as much as he used to follow his brother, and wanted to be like his brother, found his voice, as well as his strength, when it came to joining the gang life. He was particularly adamant about the initiation exercise of holding a beer bottle between his teeth while another inductee stood to the side, aimed a gun at the bottle, and fired!

He drew the proverbial line in the sand, when he boldly proclaimed, "Fuck this shit!" and announced, "Y'all ain't gotta worry about me wit all the other secrets, but I ain't down wit this bullshit...I'm out!" and threw down his flag, turned in his firearm and left the meeting place to go practice some new moves on his dirt-bike. His brother ran behind him, to warn of the dangers of leaving an initiation, but Yaz just threw up a "fuck you" sign and squeezed threw the wooden fence of Miss Gloria's yard, next to the garage, that housed his dirt bike.

At 12 years old, Yazzing's passion wasn't gang banging like Wizzard's; his greatest passion was popping wheelies on his self-purchased dirt bike, and becoming a respected, "12 O'CLOCK boy," *[one of the avid dirt bike riders skilled in the technique of making their bike suspend in a vertical position while being fully operated.]*

His next passion was to be a rapper. An aspiration he first displayed at the age of 4 when he made his debut rap song laced with 80% curse words. It was hilarious to say the least. The only thing funnier was his, "Oh so SERIOUS," expression as he delivered his creation. Oh yeah...the hand gestures that accompanied the rendition gave additional credence to the hilarity.

His other passion was a means to an end. He was a bonafide salesman by the age of ten! He sold anything and everything for his ***"BREAD and MEAT!"***

Popp recognized from whence he'd evolved and made Yazzing the heir to $10,000 worth of products when he closed the Oil Business.

Before Popp gifted his protege with the unexpected windfall, he was selling CD's, DVD's, incense, weed, loose-ones, and all the toiletries he could grab from BOE - for ONE money. BOE would boost items from CVS, RITE-AID, TARGET, or wherever he could scoop deodorant, toothpaste, and other cosmetics.

If Yaz was selling CD's or DVD's, he would get his hands on the latest hot-track of music, or bootleg version of the newest movie, and dub copies on the DVD burner he copped from one of Wizzard's crew members.

The crew acquired many electronic devices during their many sprees of heists. Yaz would dub the discs and label them, remembering the importance of neat and professional labeling from the flea market days. He figured the art of 2/$10 or 5/$20 still applied even though it was a different product. He was absolutely...RIGHT!!!

His grandfather made it a point for him to understand numbers. He also emphasized to Yaz, the importance of receiving your correct change after a purchase.

He learned very well how to maximize profits by buying packs of cigarettes cheap for $6 or $7/pack and selling "loose-ones" individually for $1 apiece. That's an awesome profit!!

The 50 cent socks and gloves that he sold for $1 could double his investment to keep his money (vehicle as Popp would call it) afloat, but not like the margin of loose-ones.

Selling weed gave him a different clientele and street cred but it was still awkward and riskier at that time. Plus it didn't give him the profits he expected for the trouble.

When BOE would come through with a bag or box of hot goods from the franchise he robbed, he would look to Yaz, another hustler, as a ONE-STOP-SHOP because Yaz would always say, "How much for ONE-MONEY, and don't be counting NO individual shit, cause it's ALL stolen." That would crack BOE up for a child to be so well versed in business opportunities. Plus, BOE knew STREET and understood his grandson was cut from an OLD SCHOOL cloth.

Anyway, BOE could make ONE-STOP and limit his exposure selling stolen goods; Yaz could maximize his profits by bargaining BOE down to the most feasible and lowest cash price. Sometimes he'd negotiate the absolute lowest price and throw in a bag of weed.

If BOE was fiending for heroin, Yaz would negotiate the lowest ONE-MONEY price, send BOE to his brother for the heroin and give his brother two or three of Wizzard's favorite deodorants or body wash.

He was very shrewd to be so young! When Popp contemplated dissolving the inventory from BNB Oils, he kept the essential products and those customers and chose Yazzings shrewdness as heir apparent to benefit from the windfall!

It was a win-win situation that not only benefited Yaz, it established him as the new big brother. He used the proceeds to help his mom pay bills. He bought school clothes for his two younger sisters ERRICKA and AEKIRA. He purchased sneakers, cell phones, video games for the entire family and even graced his mom with a gold necklace with her name on it. MYONA!

He showed all manners of responsibility and he even came in at a reasonable hour to do homework, if it wasn't already done, when he finished practicing on his dirt bike.

His windfall and development in the hierarchy couldn't have come at a better time; the newly elected Mayor was successful in getting Wiz a juvenile LIFE sentence for the incident near the mall. The case mostly pivoted around the reckless endangerment to others and proximity of the stray bullets to the same. The rival was grazed but that's a different focus point for the authorities. They really didn't care who was in the altercation, or shoot-out, if it was between gang members.

Yaz truly matured into an assertive entrepreneur; an expansive difference from the shy, reserved follower that ran around the flea market, emulating his brother, 8 years ago.

# 3rd Quarter

## Work Hardest

## Play Hardest

Another nickel truly revealed how far apart the kinfolk's paths had individualized.

Although, the children weren't exactly raised in the same house, per se; they were reared with the same tutelage. Interestingly, each individual carried Oldman's Wizardry into the industry of their choice; and each individual seemed to harness, as well as, Master the Craft of: Upholding, Demonstrating, and Perpetuating the "Jewells of Wisdom" bestowed upon them.

It was certainly a gamble teaching children so young,.. the Universal Laws and practices. Consequently, The Sage often wondered..."What *will become of these young Alchemists?"*

*

"ZING", as Yaz now prefers to be called, had his own personalized LABEL- "BTH" - ***BORN TO HUSTLE!"*** He sold: T-shirts, caps, riding gloves and his own self - produced DVD's.

He gained National notoriety for being the first "**12 O'CLOCK Boy**" to develop a stunt dubbed "**NO HANDS ZING!!!**"

A quote from one of the magazine articles written about him said, *"It was truly a dazzling display of courage and entertainment to see his blacked out bike with gold lettering spelling out "Z-I-N-G", riding down the blocked off parkway of spectators with a handsome, charismatic, innovator, garbed in his own clothing line; advertising {BTH: NO HANDS ZING!!} and riding a bike "ON- 12" with NO HANDS!!!"*

Bikers and enthusiasts came down from Philly and up from DC, and Virginia to Bodymore; to witness and participate in the festivities on Sundays.

There were music artists and movie producers amongst the spectators scouting for their company's brands; and some even enjoyed related activities. The 'event' brought out motorcycle clubs, scooter clubs, {bicycle - '12 O'Clock Boys}, and even sports car clubs! Oh yeah...the spectacle brought out police officers: in helicopters; on bicycles; on motorcycles; and in patrol cruisers.

There were *Cute, Pretty, Beautiful and Gorgeous*® {ZINGS: on- line magazine} women of all ages in the shortest shorts your heart desired.

Ohhh, there was plenty to observe and enjoy when the riders were out! There were even some female bikers!!

The *Ceautieous* were phat as shit in every dimension: tall ones, short ones; thick and thin ones; light to dark ones; rich to poor ones!

Children 5 and under were usually atop someone's shoulders unless they were in strollers. The kids atop the shoulders probably had a favorite '12 O'clock Boy' they dragged their parents out to see!

'ZING' and his stunt definitely captured the interest and envy of all who attended. The "NO-HANDS" performance was a highlight at each event. You could see several kids emulating ZING'S posture and angles on the bike and road as he whisked by them. Some kids rode their bicycles along the procession, while others copied ZING'S moves, using gestures on imaginary bicycles. They even turned their wrists like they were revving the throttle, and making sounds that resembled the actual dirt bike; "EIRNHHHH!!:. EIRNH - EIRNHH!!; EIRNH - EIRNHH - EIRNHHH!!!"

Some of the locals were selected by the moguls to perform in shows, videos and even movies. Scouts found a plethora of talent amongst the riders and signed them with big name artist while others were killed in tragic murder plots.

One year, 3 of the biker boys with promising careers were unfortunately murdered, and coincidently, were up and coming rap artists. One biker was even shot in front of his family at a family reunion. Another was chased into a Chinese Food store and riddled with bullets. Thank GOD; one survived his bullet wound to his head; while another wasn't as fortunate. They ...were brother's!!!

.40 Cal: "Her nephew was killed with one; and she didn't like it !!

ZING - didn't want to be owned, sabotaged, or murdered!! He chose to remain his own BOSS despite various interviews. His wisdom and entrepreneurial savvy paid off. He resisted being signed to the big-named labels. He truly enjoyed being sponsored and invited to California, Atlanta, Florida and Texas to display his talent.

Jealousy and envy became the normal climate in a city with a 'crab-in-a-barrel' mentality. As sure as every emotion attracts its object, ZING was a MAGNET for haters.

He was an A+ student at the local high school; a high scoring point guard; a biker boy; a devoted mate; a thugs brother; a diva's son; an activists son; an O.G.'s grandson; a hustler; a responsible big brother; a loved family member; and a respected, enlightened human.

The young and older women loved it; the dudes hated it!

The plots seemed to never stop! One opportunistic scheme seemed to prove successful. Zing ran out of gas on the revered East-side while riding one of his bikes through the projects after leaving an exhibition. The thugs, recognizing who it was, and that he was alone, and his reputed, hard-hitting brother was still locked up, seized the opportunity like a den of lions that caught a gazelle trapped in their lair. Five kids with guns threatened his life and seized the bike as a trophy.

The kids may have threatened his life, but didn't really want the reprisal to come back on their entire family. They just took the bike and didn't render any harm.

Zing on the other hand, had a laissez faire attitude. He knew and understood the culture that his pedigree was raised in and was content to leave with his health and life intact. He felt like the bike was a material possession and could be replaced.

He escaped most other plots, after he remembered his tutelage; namely, say the Lord's Prayer before you go anywhere.

One escape involved an attempt to carjack one of his vehicles. Now,.. for his '**Bread and Meat**,' he sold cars; used ones! His specialty was HONDA coupes. His mentors showed him that State law allowed 5 title changes a year without owning a car lot, even though he had aspirations of doing just that as part of his real property investments. He was very focused to be a State licensed 18 year old!

The carjack attempt came after an internet prospect arranged to meet for a sale. Zing became very private about his financial transactions so he visited his appointments alone. Popp taught all his brood the importance of an exit strategy and *"Being ready keeps you from getting ready"*

He backed into a slotted parking space near the exit of a Burger King. He immediately identified an eeriness!

55

.40 Cal: "Her nephew was killed with one; and she didn't like it !!

The reason he was so attuned to subtle energies was because Popp made a game where he would blindfold each kid and place them in the middle of a circle. Then he would spin them several rotations clockwise and reverse the process a few rotations to disorient the senses. Next he would challenge them to magnetically sense their cardinal directions: North, South, East, and West; as well as sense which family member stepped inside the circle representing their auric field. Zing proved exceptional in identifying directions as well as family members. So he was one of the best at trusting his gut feelings.

He began searching for threatening signs when the prospect was late and didn't answer his call. Grandpop taught them a magical prayer to recite at the first sign of enemies. He referred to the moment as ASA: as soon as.

So Zing began pronouncing the Spell aloud:

## SAINTS AND ANCIENTS

*Saints and Ancients form as ONE!!*
*Stretch your chords to reach this SON!!*

*Combine your FORCES in this hour*
*BLESS his WISDOM, STRENGTH and POWER*

*Saint and Ancients, flow like waters*
*Instruct the Gods, include!.. the daughters!*

*BREAK! the curses, the curses broken*

.40 Cal: "Her nephew was killed with one; and she didn't like it !!

*SPEAK! the verses, the verses spoken*

*In these 12 verses, you break all curses*
*DO IT! as I whip up this rhyme!!*

*Families are firstes, enemies get hearses*
*Remember this EV-E-RY time!!*

*Restore all our riches, defeat Ancient Witches*
*Never we victims of crime!!*

*UNTIE! Angel voices, DESTROY! demon forces*
*All others tie up with a bind!*

*[#333- When this Angel number shows itself to you, begin to say this prayer and the other 143,999 will hear you initiating prayer #333 and join your prayer to form collective Angel voices!]*

With that, ZING rubbed his palms together like people do when they're about to pull the handles on a slot machine. It was a habit he developed when his mom was bringing his favorite meal to the table.

Just then, he noticed a 2 door Honda coupe with tinted windows and Delaware license plates riding past the Burger King and entering the BP gas station across McCulloh St.

He felt an eeriness which compelled him to watch the behavior in the rear view mirror. The vehicle stopped near the air pump but no one got out and pumped air, plus the visible tires didn't need air.

A movement in his peripheral view caught his attention. Another tinted coupe made a south turn on a northbound-ONE WAY-street and turned into the same gas station. This vehicle had North Carolina tags. The dark gray coupe with NC tags slot parked in front of the convenience portion of the gas station and no one got out of that vehicle either.

Zing had seen enough and remembered Popp said, *"If you wanna be sure if someone is following/plotting you... drive the wrong way on a (ONE WAY) street."*

From his strategic position in the first parking slot near the exit, he could see about 10 blocks straight down the northbound street. He was actually located where the street bent like an elbow as it continued northward. Two of the 5 exits out of the gas station across the street were on McCulloh St which was the northbound elbowed street. One exit on each part of the arm; if the black coupe was part of a plot, it would have to exit near the air pump at the Gold St. exit to follow Zing once he blasted out of the parking lot and down McCulloh St.

Zing scanned the area for police, then studied the light sequences and the rate at which the cars were coming towards him.

"SKRRRRR" said the wheels when he peeled down the right side of McCulloh St. passing Mrs. Reed's house.

The ONE WAY drive was a short risk to Gold St., it only had six townhouses at that part of the bend from Burger King.

.40 Cal: "Her nephew was killed with one; and she didn't like it !!

Without a doubt the two suspicious cars conjoined to exit the gas station from the Gold Street exit, a half-block away from where Zing bolted. Zings' timing {PRAISE ELOHIM} was perfect to have the northbound wave of traffic cause a barrier between the coupes and Zing's exit.

His knowledge of the neighborhood allowed him the advantage of escape. He had a three block head start when he noticed the team cross McCulloh St. He made a quick right to flee up the unusually empty part of Division St. to North Ave. where he took a risky HAIL MARY to enter the main east-west thoroughfare. It had to be the grace bestowed on him from his prayer, because he was able to make the crossing with a big enough lead to vanish from his hunters before he made a quick right on Woodbrook and an immediate right turn at the fork onto Whitelock St. and left on Eutaw St. to catch the upcoming Fallsway to the highway.

He was grateful to have been taught how and when to pray. He also had a glimpse into his family's philosophy of "Shoot first; ask questions later."

Although Popp in his fifties, denounced his own tutelage of, *"You'd rather be caught with one; than without one",* regarding firearms; Zing figured, it may be time he adopted the street policy.

Continuing up the Fallsway, he reflected on numerous lessons. The Parkway was the first place Popp took him to drive on the Highway.

.40 Cal: "Her nephew was killed with one; and she didn't like it !!

The lesson was for him to study the Jersey wall and all the marks upon them. *Popp explained how the marks represented how many people misjudged LIFE'S twists and turns.*"

Despite the Fallsway being an example of misperceptions, Zing chose to roll a blunt with NO HANDS on the steering wheel!

For some unexplained reason he was thee undisputed DAREDEVIL!!

**"NO HANDS ZING!!!!!"**

*

Five years in Juvie definitely didn't reform Wiz. He proved to be 10 times more knowledgeable, and 100 times more ruthless!!

Despite being a mannerly gentleman in the eyes of the staff, he was undoubtedly the most feared and treacherous juvenile amongst inmates by the time he went before Judge Stein, several months after his 18th birthday.

The Judge couldn't understand how he became an entire media sensation with his own fan club. The club created petitions and sent letters suggesting, "FREE WIZ!!"

As far as the judicial system was concerned, he was a model inmate. He was even promoted to team leader on the unit he resided.

When he went to court, Popp showed up as a character witness.

The judge began to set the framework for outlining Wizzard's printed picture as a career type criminal. Judge Stein read aloud the charges and added a skewed, biased comment to each. He overemphasized how heinous and dangerous the stray bullet was, and the effects it could've had on the driver's family.

Despite Wizzard's completion of the 5 year term, and all the commitments assigned to him throughout his tenure, the Judge kept mentioning behavior he'd done time for. The court proceedings were supposed to be determining the conditions of Wizzard's release, somehow, the discussion seemed to be centered around reasons to keep him incarcerated.

The Judge began to suggest that X-MAS was the worst time to release a young black man into the type of environment Wiz came from. He even noted a previous case where he released a 21 year old with a similar profile to his neighborhood where he was charged and the young man was murdered days after release.

Popp heard enough red lining and raised his hand for attention. When his hand was not recognized, he cleared his throat LOUDLY!!

When Judge Stein recognized the blatant gesture, he asked who he was and did he have something he wanted to say. Popp turned on his humble disposition and stood up. He cleared his throat for real and invoked the MOST HIGH to represent his grandson in this legal matter. There was no indication that the HOLY ONE had answered his prayer, because you can't feel the

.40 Cal: "Her nephew was killed with one; and she didn't like it !!

HOLY SPIRIT when it attunes to your spirit. It is as subtle as the AIR you breathe when IT indwells you. Nor did he have any idea what he was going to say, until he opened his mouth and heard, when everyone else heard, the utterance which came forth.

"*LUCIFERRR, listen to me carefully!*" Although POPP was listening to the words bellowing from the deep, dark, depths of his Spiritual Ocean, he also heard a chorus in the background of his mind chanting:

*I.M. Mortal Portal, you won't recognize M.E.*
*Not my wheels, as they turn; not my soul, Astral free!*

*I.M. Mortal Portal, veiled dimensions, will I peep:*
*I have Visions when awake; Lucid dreams, when asleep*

*I.M. Mortal Portal, DARK as MATTER, "LIFE of TREE;"*
*'KASHIC RECORDS, Seventh Heavens, distant places, Yeah,... I*
*BE!!*

*I.M. Mortal Portal, ears won't fathom, eyes can't see; but if you*
*ask...then I'll share what ARC GABE reveals to M.E.*"

*[#777- When this Angel number shows itself to you, begin to recite these words and the other 143,999 will hear you initiating prayer #777 and join your prayer to form collective Angel voices!]*

.40 Cal: "Her nephew was killed with one; and she didn't like it !!

As an unexpected breeze whisked through the courtroom, POPP continued channeling.

*"With all due respect, I Am ALEXANDER ST. ANTHONY, and WINSTON WILLIAM WHITE is my biological grandson through my daughter. I've listened and I've heard all that was said, your Honor, regarding his charges, his misdirection, and your personal experiences with the black male youth demographic coming from the impoverished neighborhoods in the city. However, I didn't hear any references made to the changes Mr. White has made during his juvenile experience within this penal system. The times I came to visit him, it was often pointed out through various staff members, how gracious and respectful he was to work with. When I spoke with his counselor Ms. Grant, I was informed he completed each of the 3-18 month commitments he signed up for. If you and the courts could allow me 2 more minutes, I'd like to close by pointing out, there's nowhere in this city where a young black male is exempt from violence or drugs. Therefore, if my grandson intends to mature to be a productive citizen, he'll have to make that decision in an environment that's indigenous to him. I thank you for your time."*

Then Popp sat down. ***For the millisecond he was seated, he began to reminis…***

.40 Cal: "Her nephew was killed with one; and she didn't like it !!

*ELOHIM; 1979- "You have two ears and one mouth; what does that mean?*

*(St.) STREET - "Listen twice as much as I talk!"*

*ELOHIM - "Correct!"*

*ELOHIM; 2011- "You have two ears and one mouth; what does that mean?*

*(St.) SAINT - "Listen twice as much as I talk!"*

*ELOHIM - "This time, hear MY voice as you speak, because the second ear will be your inner ear, and you will have to hear my VOICE and interpret my MESSAGE while you are talking. As you speak to them; I will speak to you! As your listeners hear your voice; you will have to hear my voice! After all, YOU are my ELECTED speaker, and your ears are closest to...YOUR mouth!*

While he was reflecting, the Judge said, "Mr. St Anthony, if you could stand please as I address your evocation.

[*It was like the Judge himself didn't actually realize* that *his courtroom had been warped into an enchanted dimension.*]

You obviously have observed the dynamics of your grandson's development, and I admire your insight and perspective into this unique situation. So, I want you to speak with another Judge with regards to this issue.

.40 Cal: "Her nephew was killed with one; and she didn't like it !!

*[He stood humbly, with his feet angled at 33°, and his right- hand atop his left. In his mind, he was thinking he already spoke to another JUDGE; the TRUE JUDGE]*

Would that be okay with you?" "Certainly," Popp responded. He was shocked,[ but didn't show it], that no one seemed to react to the LUCIFER salutation.

"Well fine." the Judge stated as he looked at the prosecutor and other staff in the courtroom. "I'll release him and recommend that he stay away from the neighborhood until next Friday when we return for Judge Harris to hear your perspective. Will that be okay?"

"Certainly, your Honor," Popp conceded. "Fine," the Judge concluded, "You can sign for him over there," as he pointed to the clerks desk. "Your Honor," Popp interrupted, "Maybe I didn't make myself clear." He followed by saying, "Winston is 18 now, I'm expecting, as well as encouraging him to take responsibility for the outcome of his own life!! He'll be signing to be released on his own recognizance. Is that okay with YOU Judge?"

The Judge looked over his spectacles and nodded his head in approval of what he just witnessed. "As you say," when he hammered the gavel and instructed the court.

After a few formalities he waited for his released grandson outside of the Juvenile Justice System.

Wiz, Myesha and Momo came out the door with youthful grins as if they'd won the prize fight.

Popp was quick to wipe those ridiculous grins off their faces with his tone and facial expressions as he stated, "Grandson listen to me...you've already learned to be a "G." let me teach you how to become an Old "G," so you can enjoy the pleasure of advising your grandsons one day, I pray. HALLELUJAH!"

He continued his monologue to contrite faces with, "it's a trap,..a set-up!" "These people have your pedigrees written down in docket numbers. They're betting on you going to your neighborhood where you were forbidden and regaining your previous contacts and resuming your previous behaviors. What I'm urging you to comprehend is this, 7 days of fun and reconnection are not worth the 15 years hanging over your head if you violate this 7 day order and get convicted as an adult. So grandson...please Hear me!! Stay the FUCK away from the 'M,' stay with your Shawty, get some loving, work on a master plan, get ready to come back here next Friday and get your FREEDOM!!"

Wiz looked like he grew up in a few minutes. He was already Popp's size and weight but his countenance seemed to change from a boy's to a man's!

They hugged for the first time in a long time, then dapped and went their separate ways.

66

After turning the corner he immediately began praying "***Saints and Ancients form as One…!!***" He was totally trusting the Magical Forces to protect and guide his child until he'd see him again through this tempting, upcoming week!

*

Popp was suited and early for the meeting. The early halls of the court echoed from the various types of heels clicking and clacking amidst the anticipation. Although he didn't expect his grandson to be early, he hadn't heard any news pertaining to anything contrary to him being alright. In their family dynamic, "No news, is good news," and his daughter hadn't called with any updates, so Popp would periodically peer down the long hall to see his son as he arrived.

Court was scheduled for 9:30 am and it was only 8:37 am! Cousin Angie worked in the clerk's office across the hall from the room they were expected to meet in and he hadn't checked in with her for a while so he asked the receptionist if she was available. "THANK GOD!!" He thought she wasn't one of those: gum-popping, phone-texting, breath-scoffing, receptionists, but she did just point to the left without any real directions or communication. He knew the way, and tapped on the door with the back of his knuckle.

Angie had her back turned. The neat freak was cleaning something or organizing something as usual. "Oh, hey cuz" as she turned and gave the strongest hug with those skinny arms. "Your grandson again?" She questioned with the wisdom of an owl, peering through her side glance. "Um humm" he agreed while appreciating her collection of photos from their shared branch of WATTS clan!!

"I'm not even gon' ask" speaking the family code of "DON'T ASK, DON'T TELL." If you're down here, I can imagine which one "she prophesied", still arranging and cleaning. He commented on a photo of her mother who died when she was a little girl, "Is that ELLIE?...She's beautiful cuz,...you look just like her!!" She didn't usually respond much to memories of her mom.

"I'm about to retire this year" she changed the subject. Then, it became apparent,...she was packing - not cleaning!

Just then, his grandson popped into his mind. He summarized his visit by saying, "I just wanted to stop by and holler at you!! His cousin came over and gave him a different kind of embrace. She threw her arm over his shoulders and around his neck as she said, "You always do cuz, you always do!! I want you to know, I love you for that" as she released him to his world of grandparenting.

Wiz was coming down the hall when he exited the clerk's office. He didn't have on a suit, but he had on a button down shirt with his jeans and it was tucked inside of his GUCCI belt!

He looked peaceful and rested. " You Look good", and he responded, "I've just been chillin."

Popp, Wiz and Myesha, get in line to enter the courtroom to find out the stipulations of his release. As soon as they entered, the Sheriff retrieved Popp and Wiz and ushered them to the Clerks desk where the States Attorney was waiting. She reintroduced herself and explained that Judge Harris listened to the transcript and we didn't have to wait or speak with the judge and he was free to go!

Wizzard's eyes Popped open in disbelief as he stammered when he said, "I...I...I can go?" Ms. Porshensky, couldn't help but chuckle at his response when she polited her demeanor and repeated, "YES...yes...you're free to go !"

Myesha was still climbing over people in the third to the last row; oblivious, they were done!

Popp urged Wiz to stay connected and was exiting the court when he heard a loving contrite voice pronounce, "I LOVE YOU!!" Not missing a step he loudly and clearly pronounced, "I LOVE YOU MORE, SON!!

*

Exactly 30 days after Wizzard's release. The 7:45 pm. red-light, caught a navy blue Mercedes Sedan at the corner of northbound Charles St. at North Ave. Four juveniles in a stolen painter's cargo van pulled beside the driver's side of the vehicle while two other juveniles wearing masks on dirt bikes pulled next to the passenger's side. Before the light turned green, over 40 - .40 Caliber shells sparkled beneath the cerulean blue sky. The Judge lay slumped on his horn; the car drifted, then stopped.

It was the same corner where the 21 year old who the Judge mentioned in the Court proceedings was murdered!

The executioners were only one block from the bridge that led to the expressway with the tire-stained Jersey walls!!

Three months later, at 3:33 pm., on the Summer Solstice, the rival from the mall fiasco was playing basketball at a court which was within earshot of his daughter's grandmother's house when police discovered dozens of .40 caliber shells amidst a massive pool of blood.

The guys who robbed ZING for his dirt bike, never saw the chess-move coming as they shot CRAPS in the courtyard of Latrobe projects. Mere milliseconds into the cerulean blue sky, a tractor trailer parked at the opening of the courtyard where the gang was gathered. No one noticed. Shortly thereafter, each airway or escape path was covered by soldiers flanking the exits of the alleys, but still out of perception from the targets. Wiz sent two soldiers through each of the 3 airways, as six more blitzed the courtyard from behind the trailer. When the noise, smoke, and scattering ceased, way more than 40 - .40 caliber casings twinkled under the street lights which came on during the massacre. Six bleeding bodies lie unable to hear the screaming and crying condoling their departure.

Perhaps the timing was a testament to Wizzard's expertise and calculations.

*

The police never seemed to connect the dots on the .40 caliber casings they were finding amongst the various precincts, but there was one neighborhood that knew WHY, and all the surrounding neighborhoods knew WHO was running THAT neighborhood!

It was a very busy year for Wizzard. He'd escaped 3 different murder attempts and impregnated 3 different women.

One attempt on his life resulted in Wiz getting grazed between his thighs as he was scurrying from his assailant. Another time, one of his enemies must've recognized him at the gas station. He spint the bend and was able to stab Wiz in the side when he caught him putting the credit card into the pump. He was even able to escape a barrage of bullets that hailed into the RANGE ROVER he bought for Myesha.

He was truly personifying his nickname. Folks started speculating. Especially folks who never saw the power of prayer, and didn't understand that all of ELOHIM'S Archangels are Angels of Death; not to be misconstrued for DEATH ANGELS {bloodthirsty warmongers}. At least, if he wasn't a wizard, perhaps his grandfather was, they would say; or at best, a fervent pray-er, and the funny thing about it, that's exactly who nicknamed him Wizzard!

*

Cherokee's path couldn't be more far removed from the nephew who is 3 days her junior. Her cousin Shaun- the NUMEROLOGIST, says, "It's all in the numbers." His chosen path did not affect their bond one bit. She understood his motives and bitterness more than anyone else. Was it because their bond was miraculously formed in the exact same nursery bed, that they shared so much in common; but how would that explain the unique bond with the other brother who was 18 months younger?

The patriarch will never forget the ominous day at Johns Hopkins Hospital when he was leaving the unit with his youngest bundle of JOY. As he was walking through the hall after 3 exasperating days, he recognized his oldest bundle of joy waddling towards the obstetrics unit he was leaving.

Her face was swollen and distressed as she was rushing towards relief. All her father could say was, "I'll be right back."

By the time he got his wife and family settled so he could return to the aid of his first born, the new granddad's older sister - POO POT - was performing REIKI on the newborn. As soon as he entered the room she passed him his first grandchild.

The interesting thing he remembered, when he removed the swaddling from over the baby's face, the newbie reached up, grabbed the blanket and pulled it back down over its face.

Day ONE, an enlightened grandfather knew this individual would be a powerful force to contend with.

The next omen came later that evening when the nurse returned him to the nursery. Popp realized he was also placed in the same bed as his aunt - #2225. "What are the chances?" he thought, **"You Can't Make This Stuff Up!!"** [YCMTSU]

Not being adept enough to read those signs at 34 years old, Popp conceded, after trying to demystify the coincidence, that the mystery had something to do with the criss-crossing of their life-paths.

Here it is, 18-19 years later, and their paths couldn't be more opposite. He's become a felon of extraordinary acclaim, while she's graduated and attending college.

Nevertheless, her big brother/nephew is the core of her heart, regardless of his misdirection. Since childhood, she's defended his misunderstood actions; so she reasoned.

While he was incarcerated, she would visit, leave money, accept phone calls, and make sure he had, at least, one of her girlfriends as a pen pal. When he was home, she would have sleepovers to ensure he had access to a variety of her friends.

Cherokee had ONE awkward advance on the bus-stop one day she was going to school. Wiz heard about it in juvie and from there had the boy beat up at the same spot where his aunt was so-called disrespected!

It was because of her nephew that the seed of becoming a lawyer was spawned! She had an uncanny ability to understand how the misdirection performed.

She was also a natural for the field of Psychology. Because of that insight, she felt she would better serve mankind and the disenfranchised if she became a lawyer.

However harmonic the triad's familial bond, their life-paths may have something in common, but their chosen paths seem to have nothing in common except family!

With regards to the "TWIN- MOUNTAINS", one of Cherokee's nephews was locally infamous, the other was nationally famous. She felt humble in the spotlight, and secure between the personification of the 'Mountains' prophecy.

She was plowing her way through the traps, temptations, and pitfalls of a city with a - crab in a barrel - mentality; but somehow, she seemed relentlessly focused, as she was the embodiment of her father's *wise sayings*. She spouted his proverbs and axioms with fluidity. She was indubitably the daughter every father would be proud of. Her INTUITION was remarkable! Her inclinations and proclivities were so much like her fathers, she could only be rightly guided! And she knew it!!

At college, plenty of freshmen take the first year of autonomy to goof off, Cherokee was no different, but it didn't take long before she buckled down and focused on the mission at hand.

Focusing on the mission required her to *Balance the opposing fish!!* *Both PISCES were always grinding to make the cash, but they had to be on their respective 'A-games' when it came to balancing their individual dual-sided personalities. His ass was a bonafide JEKYLL - HYDE; period!!*

*She, on the other hand:*

- *1. Newly graduated - BLACKBELT*
- *2. Knife throwing - EXPERT*
- *3. Binge watcher of anything WEAPON!*
  *on the other;*
- *1. licensed Insurance provider*
- *2. Has 2 degrees; Law, Business*
- *3. Killing the game with her business model*

*She took her catchphrase, and clothing line-**CPBG**-*
*CUTE, PRETTY, BEAUTIFUL, GORGEOUS, into a GAME SHOW!!*

*She catapulted her Real Estate Firm - **BREEZY ESTATES LLC d/b/a FREA and CLEER PROPERTIES** into the operating arm of her Charity - **FOUNDATION for SINGLE MOTHERS.***

Perhaps, she and Zing have more in common, with regards to business, than they previously paid attention to.

Popp often wondered if he ruined the kids by starting them as entrepreneurs at such an early age. He was convinced that the wisdom they possessed as teenagers was as dangerous as a gun in the hands of a toddler. He wanted to make sure his kids had a viable skill to succeed in this hard world, but always remembered what Little Kenny {one of his mentees} told him after making enough money at the age of sixteen to buy a car; " I can sell anything. I could sell snow to an Eskimo!" That may have sounded really cute, and confident, but the only snow he ended up selling was cocaine and heroin, which left an indelible impression on the senior; ...not a good one. The revelation actually had him thinking about ending the mentoring program; however, when he noticed the entrepreneurial aptitude of his younger brood, he couldn't resist teaching them the craft!

When it pertained to her nephews, Cherokee had a unique position in the family hierarchy. For her, one nephew was more like a big brother that warned and threatened their peers.

The other little brother/nephew allowed her to dote, boss, and mother; maybe that's the same thing, maybe not. She approved or disapproved of his prospects. She stayed in his ass about family - RULES - over all that other fleeting - BULLSHIT!! She would recite adages, maxims, and proverbs to him when she caught him glamorizing on Social Media or putting his image too far out in certain neighborhoods. She would remind him they were taught, *"FORTUNE is wiser than FAME!!*

When she wasn't mothering, she certainly was supporting his various business ventures: when she needed new fashion,..YUP!!, he set his only girlfriend up with a cute little boutique; when she needed her nails done,.. yup!!, he set his cousin up after she graduated from nail school. Cherokee would buy her "ICEY WATER" from ZINGS little brother; set up near the park! ZING philosophized that if he froze the waters and thawed them out as he was setting ERRICK up, he could give his customers the chill they desired in a beverage on a sweltering day!!

She would support her nephew if he was doing a Fashion-shoot at the park, or a show featuring one of his latest hits!!

She would be the first to let him know if a design was gonna - POP- or DROP!!

She marveled at the insulation between her two 'SONS', as she called them. The advantages of having two nephews her age far outweighed the disadvantages. She had the respect, clout, protection, and favor that caused any young woman to envy her.

YEAHH! Young Cherokee was living her BEST LIFE!

.40 Cal: "Her nephew was killed with one; and she didn't like it !!

\*

Myesha proved to be an extremely faithful soldier; krazy, no doubt, but the key word is SOLDIER!! Her natural pedigree, combined with Wizzard's tutelage, groomed her to become a terrible force to contend with. Most people in the streets believed she was the invisible arms of the Wizzard while he was away.

Their cute little courtship started in middle school. One day, a couple of months after the school year began, a handsome, well groomed new classmate sat at the seat in the corner of room #222. Myesha chewed her gum, and filed her nails, as she usually did. From her diagonal position from his corner, she noticed him. His dozing head slipped out of the pillow, his cupped-hand made. He scanned the room to see if anyone noticed him dozing or jerking and zeroed straight into her admiring eyes. He paid very little attention to the admiration and proceeded to doze back off instead of suffering the boring teacher.

He was re-awakened when the adjacent desk bumped up against the desk he was resting on. Myesha deliberately caused the jolt when she pulled out the chair to sit next to her future beau, as she imagined.

He was gracious and cavalier, assuming it was haphazard. He casually slid his desk a few inches from the desk Myesha now occupied and returned to his position on his hand. He reasoned it to be a good mistake because he now had the wall to assist in bracing him from the next jerk.

The next interruption came when the teacher asked Myesha, "Myesha is that your seat?" and she rebutted with "Mr. Taylor, you know I sit wherever I want, stop trippin!"

Wiz literally opened one eye to witness where all this audacity was coming from. Still believing this whole fiasco was part of the normal classroom dynamics, he was shocked to see a well dressed, hair did, recalcitrant, staring in his face, with the chair turned towards him as if he was about to be interviewed by Oprah.

Her lips were pursed, and she seemed to be impatient to get this interview started. Her gaze into his soul was fixed. She waited for him to respond so she could begin her interview. He didn't. He was about to allow that one opened eye to rejoin the closed eye when he heard a piercing, raspy voice with a turned up octave ask, "Where you come from?" To him, it didn't seem like she was asking, it seemed like she was demanding. Nevertheless, he said, "Down the bottom, Shawty." "Down the bottom... where?" she insisted, like some kind of class bully. Wiz sat up, and took inventory of the classroom dynamics, only to realize she was the class bully, and everyone, even the teacher, was waiting for a response from the new kid on the block.

Wiz was a leader and was impressed with a female version of himself. He thought she would make a good gang moll to keep the other women in check, as well as some of the dudes. He knew all eyes were on him and decided to slay the whole class with his status in one fell swoop, when he confidently responded, "If I tell you, I'll have to kill you!" The entire class was lit up with various responses. Mr. Taylor assured the new kid was raised by the old breed, and surmised this kid could be more than meets the eye; he instantly knew this kid was a force to contend with! Some of the kids from down the bottom, boys and girls, knew he must be ganged up. Others who didn't know the streets thought he was either a comedian or quick witted. Myesha thought, "This could be my baby-daddy!" He maintained her gaze until it turned into a side glance as she exited the out turned chair to return to her assigned seat at the opposite corner of the classroom. Although she didn't respond to his quick wit, you couldn't notice her wheels as they turned in her mind.

The next turn-on came during gym class. The boys were playing basketball, and Wiz was coming down the court with the ball. Another class semi-bully was being a little over zealous about stealing the ball and kept body bumping him in the attempts. After a few excessive attempts, Wiz mushed him; he took his outspread hand, grabbed the boy's whole face, and pushed him straight-arm style, to the floor, and continued to take the lay-up.

After the lay up was made, Wiz turned around and leaped over the fallen on his way up the court with total disregard for the reprisal. Myesha, studying from the side-line, had been forthrightly watching her prospect all day, and saw each and every disposition the new kid was displaying and also what he wasn't displaying. The way Wiz handled the other bully, she knew he was the ONE for her.

At the end of the school day, the kids were all at their assigned lockers. Not Myesha!! She's slamming the open locker next to Wizzards to assure she'd get his attention. He asked her, "Shawty whatchu want wit me? I'm not who you think I am." She said, " Shut up! You don't know what I think, and I don't give a damn who you are!" Perplexed, he wanted to know why she was exerting so much energy in his direction, and asked, "Well, why you keep pushing up on me? I don't want no trouble, Shawty!!" "First," she said, with her ponytail swanging, and her head bobbing, "My name is NOT-SHAWTY!! It's Myeeesha.!" as she changed her tone to a sultry one; who would've thought? "Next" she said, "I THINGKK, I'm gonna make you my man!!" He held back the majority of his laugh, but some of the hilarity oozed through his crooked smile when he smirkily said, "I don't want to be your boyfriend!" She took one step closer, while pointing her right {serious}index finger towards his comprehension, as she said," I said,... MAN!!" He realized the class bully was serious and responded, "I don't want no girlfriend right now Shawty." Wiz made the mistake of turning towards his locker when he rejected Myesha's advance. She leaped on his back, choking him in a half nelson and said, "You think I'm playing with you?" The wrestler slid out of her hold, cavalierly of course, and assured her, "I'm impressed with your little proposal!" He blushed, and looked over his shoulder only to see her waving her fist at him, and telepathically meaning "You better be my boyfriend/man or I'll harass the shit out of you!!" And the rest, as they say is...His-story, or her-story, depends on who you ask!!

Now she's pregnant, and dealing with sociopath dramas.

He was already:  a Big Boy, a Hot boy, and a Dope boy, before Myesha's southern connection made him a Gun-boy!!

He was buying wholesale cases of .40 calibers, and ammunition. His distribution consisted of,...well...every bad-boy in the town.  He was locally infamous within all the gang groups, and not one street kid broke the code to the authorities. Also, it may have had something to do with his one rule;

RULE #1- "If you say my name, you'll get 40-.40's"

No one seemed to doubt it.  It certainly had been demonstrated, on numerous occasions.  It didn't seem to be politically correct according to gangland standards, but the way he brokered the firearms left him with various non-partisan alliances.

His alliances afforded:  peace-treaties, drug deals, and other minor resolutions that didn't require guns.  So, his newfound status only added insult to injury, when it came to Myesha dealing with the backlashes of his infamy.

Myesha's INSULTS included her: dignity, pride, ownership, devotion, and trust. They were all centered around his infidelity,  and emotional abuse.

.40 Cal: "Her nephew was killed with one; and she didn't like it !!

The INJURIES to Myesha consisted of:  family alienation; lost two apartments;  3 cars shot up; 2 black eyes; several bruised arms; one broken finger and Oh Yeah! Several broken hearts!

Her dramas or more or less, his dramas imposed on her, consist of:  a murder investigation; at least, one, street contract; 2 other baby-mamas; she also has a gun charge; her family hates him; and her girlfriend suspects Wiz of having her daughter's father killed.

Yet, in the midst of all the Chaos, she still rides with her MAN! FOR NOW!

*

When Popp and Nanna met at the hospital on the day of Myesha's delivery, they both had on those blue and green Rugby Polo shirts. Myesha's mom Starr, joked [or was serious] about how coonish the two old people looked all dressed alike.  They didn't care.  They sat snuggled on the guest couch waiting for their first great-grandchild!

Popp was Wizzard's grandfather{Wiz was POPP'S first grandchild} and Nanna was Myesha's grandmother, {Myesha was NANNA'S first grandchild}. They'd been seeing each other since Myesha's graduation.

After Wiz got out of Juvie, Popp and Myesha became really tight.  She enjoyed his wisdom; and antics; he respected her strength and loyalty.  So, when Myesha was graduating, she summoned Popp that "He'd better be there"

83

or he would have to answer to her. She even arranged for him to pick up the ticket from her grandmother.

He made it there, but he was late! He'd talked with Myesha before she left for the Graduation, and promised attendance. When he arrived at the gate and realized he'd forgotten his phone; Myesha's class was already seated in the large football field. She must've been watching and waiting because she performed some kind of symbol that let her grandma know that Wizzards grandfather was at the gate. The grandmother handed the ticket to one of the other grandkids to take to the man at the gate.

At the gate, the kid turned around and ran back to "wherever" before Popp got through the gate, so he wasn't able to identify which party he should be joining.

While looking for a vacancy amongst the seats at the bleachers an attractive young lady flagged him in the direction of her party. Popp thought, "The lady with the expensive sandals must be Myesha's mother." He sat in the midst of the party; one bench behind the Nubian braided beauty.

No one else acknowledged him because they were all tuned in to the commencements.

From 10 feet away from the young sandaled Goddess, he whispered, "You have beautiful feet and coyly turned away as if he didn't say it.

He held the con momentarily by pretending to be people watching in the other direction. He had his boyish innocent face on display when he heard, "What did you say?" in a firm, distinct, proper voice.

When he turned around, she looked straight in his eyes and demanded, "Did you say something to me?" He knew instantly where Myesha got her gruff. He flipped the con when he said, "Huh?" Excuse me! Were you talking to me?" She repeated herself, "I asked you, did you just say something to me?" He leaned up on the bench and poked his chest forward and forged through the challenge as he toned down his con and softened his voice and lowered his eyes and said, "I think your feet are perfect!" in his RICO-SUAVE voice. As intensely as he zoomed into his skit; he zoomed out, and zoomed into the graduation.

By the time that day was over, they'd gone go-cart riding; bistro dining; and were saying goodnight with a kiss.

They'd been together everyday since, and now they're waiting to share a great grandchild.

*

Popp and Wiz left the delivery room. Along the corridor, they were careful not to speak open-air. When Wiz saw the nurse enter the echoed corridor, he asked his grandfather had he seen the terrace yet; suggesting a nice place to converse. Popp simply smiled and said nothing until the nurse passed.

.40 Cal: "Her nephew was killed with one; and she didn't like it !!

He shrugged his lip denoting, "That's fine!"

They turned into the elevator lobby, and were surprised by Wolf and Seven as they disembarked from the elevator. Wolf is POPP'S only son, and Seven is Wolf's only son. Wolf asked where they were going, and the two were simultaneously answering while Wolf was asking, "The Terrace?"

They all laughed, even Seven!

The terrace was the glass door adjacent to the lobby and you could see the skyline, and whoever was on the deck, through the window from the lobby. Halfway out into the garden, big Winston was giving Zing a lecture.

Popp thought this to be ominous because he also intended to give the young men the fruits of his experiences. He wasn't sure what he was witnessing, as Winston was making urgent arm gestures waving the guys to his cause.

When they arrived, Winston exasperatingly pleaded, "Please help me!! Maybe...one of yall can get through his hardhead!"

Popp, assumed the usual when he dragged Winston to the side and admonished him.

The first thing Popp asked Winston was, "Do you see yourself? Do you really...see...yourself?" Then he reminded him how "KNOW-IT-ALLSEY" he was when he got 30 years with the Feds, and just got out after 19 years. He assured Winston that the men he called sons had chosen their paths years ago!! Popp wanted to give Winston the best advice for his unique circumstance, and

86

suggested, "The best thing you can probably do with them now is erase the chronological age out of your equation. You'll have to accept that "TWIN MOUNTAINS" have forged in an environment that is indigenous to them!!

That's when Winston pleaded, "Can you say something to him then?"

Popp had mosied up the terrace and was nodding his head to let Wolf know he was next. When he heard Winston's plea, he cut his eyes in his direction and confirmed that he heard with an extra nod.

All of the brood had been so busy, Popp hadn't seen any of the boys for a while. He squoze and squoze his son as he congratulated his selection of service. He assured Wolf he was continually changing when he said, "I'm proud of myself son. My therapy gave me the insight; that I never was a WHORE!! I was DYSFUNCTIONAL and I tried to make a collage of attributes total up to one woman. Anyway, nevermind all that psycho mumbo jumbo, I only date one woman at a time now!! And I'm so proud!! Although...I will give her ass a two year probationary period." They laughed, then gave each other -5- for being a 'GOOD DUDE', but not a damn fool!

*

Wiz knew he was next and was reading the body language. Popp was able to literally do an-about face-and turn right into his "WHOL-E-HEART", which was only one of the Shamanic names he dubbed his first-born grandchild.

.40 Cal: "Her nephew was killed with one; and she didn't like it !!

They had way too much to catch up on and way too little time to do it!

ONE-SUN walked the Patriarch all the way to the end of the terrace where the ambient noise was traffic,16 floors below!

Before {TWIN MOUNTAINS; at least, one of them } could debrief, his {REAL-ONE; ANCIENT EAGLE} exhorted him! *"Hell has no fury like a woman scorned!"*

In anticipation of the Wisdom he was about to receive, the first-time father barely heard the sprinkled JEWELLS, "Huh? What'd you say?" First-time Great-Granddad repeated, with a more prophesying tone!!

"CHEROKEE WARRIOR!!!!!"NO -fucking-doubt!!; 5Star-CANNON!! outa O!K!-KO-RAL!!, yet still!!,...should pearls be cast to the swine?"

It's a Prophet's duty to speak the words although the listener may or may not receive Wisdom from "THE ANCIENT of DAYS!"

This young man had way too much on his mind for prophetic babbling, and food certainly wasn't one of the most important things when he told Popp he was putting a McDonald's bag in his backpack in case he got hungry later on. The senior agreed, "Sure."

Youngbuck got close and told Ole-man about his windfall of artillery and asked his Sage for clarity on his "GOOD FORTUNE." Wise-one reminisced about a prayer he said one of the times FIRSTBORN got shot. He told his "ONE- Under-Da-Sun" that when he prayed for his PROTECTION &

.40 Cal: "Her nephew was killed with one; and she didn't like it !!

SECURITY he got an unexpected package delivered to the wrong address. "You know ELOHIM works in MYSTEEEERIOUS ways!!" he interjected!

It was a bulletproof vest...in Wizzard's size! **Fortunate for him because he was beefing with a rival gang when the Miracle arrived!**

He reminded grandson it was some time ago when he brought him the vest. Actually, it was during the time Popp was summoned down-south, when ELOHIM introduced HIS PRESENCE to him.

He began to drift down *memor...*

*Popp had to go down South on some family matters! While down-south, he met a cutie! She introduced him to her family as an angel; he wasn't aware of her psychic abilities yet, nor was he aware that the majority of the people in the town had special gifts. He deduced his Purpose for her family and set out to do what he felt he was summoned to do for her family! They were looking for a rental unit in a rough hood! A car pulled up! The driver cried out! "Hey!!How you guys doing? Need a ride?"*

*The two looked at each other with a "split- decision!" One thing led to another; they got in the back of the car!! The dude " DONUT-R.I.P" askt their names!*

*Jessie - said, " Jessie Maeee!" in her Southern drawl!*

*Popp - said, " E - LO - HIM!", but YOU can call me E-LO !" in a stern, authoritative tone!*

.40 Cal: "Her nephew was killed with one; and she didn't like it !!

*They looked at each other in another split-decision! He shrugged his*
*shoulders!*

*He'd never heard the name before, which proceeded from his depths!*
*They handled their business! Jessie took E-LO to the library! He did his*
*research, and discovered the Creator of Heaven and Earth heard his prayer*
*and confirmed it through his very own being!*

*[He'd askt GOD to accompany him down south in his prayer before he*
*boarded the plane!]*

*He started dancing!!!!! and Praise!!! in the library, and NOT one*
*person in the entire library of Hopkinsville Kentucky lifted a head!!*

*Astounding, amazing, and magical, he thought!!*

*Since THAT experience, zillions of Supernatural occurrences happen*
*in HIS PRESENCE now!!*

A millisecond later, the doorway to vision world closed, and he returned
to reality on the roof deck!!

An epiphany occurred to the Sage, and the 'Descendant of the Ancients'
surmised the artillery to be the "SECURITY" part of the prayer if the vest
represented the PROTECTION! He conjectured to his mentee, because GOD
works in  mysterious ways,..DEDUCTION - will be the tool that unravels

.40 Cal: "Her nephew was killed with one; and she didn't like it !!

those mysteries. Right now, the Theosophist deduced, it was ELOHIM'S signature all over this Mystery.

While the senior was resonating from the Majical feelings associated with the experience down-south, an inquisitive voice says,"I really don't understand what makes things happen the way they do when you're around, but it's working!" Surprisingly, he had the most unassuming look upon his human/angelic face. Nevertheless, he was truly enamored with the amazing way things happened in his Grand's Presence!

"Well,...let me give it to you in a language that you WILL comprehend," the hierophant de-mystified.

"You see, grandson", the Theosophist theologized, "**FAITH is like a .40 Cal.; and WISDOM is its bullet!!!**

*[As they share a birdseye view over the entire city landscape!!]*

Grandson peered over the town with his progenitor thinking, "There he goes with that analogy shit!!, but knowing from experience, he'd better take heed!

"The Secret that makes a Master Theosophist" he continued, "is having the WISDOM to know W-H-E-N to pull the trigger of FAITH. Knowing W-H-E-N to pull the trigger of FAITH creates a different caliber weapon that aims more accurately at its target, which, in this analogy,... IS 'things HOPED for.' Plus, the rule is the same for the wicked and the Righteous.

.40 Cal: "Her nephew was killed with one; and she didn't like it !!

The HOPE or DESIRE that enters into your spirit is a complete entity when it arrives in your consciousness. Any image or WORD you receive in your Mortal Consciousness from the LIVING GOD is already WHOLE and COMPLETE and doesn't require your limited mentality to validate its authenticity. Our Creator **CAN NOT create an unfinished: Thought, Idea, Vision, Desire, or anything for that matter.**

Knowing W-H-E-N to pull the trigger of FAITH is more powerful than merely having FAITH, as most people assume. "HAVING FAITH " in a crisis, is as futile as having a firearm in your possession and not knowing w-h-e-n to use it to protect yourself in your most urgent need for victory. In Martial Arts, according to BRUCE LEE, [*Thinking he could appeal to the pugilist*] Speed and Accuracy equals Power! In Spiritual warfare, you need to speedily and accurately identify the cancerous threat of DOUBT!!, or any of its known associates, and judo-flip doubt into belief."

[*He ends dramatically, and with a full demonstration*]

Wiz held back the hardest grin from his favorite storyteller!

"The reference to pulling the trigger is a perfect analogy expressing how instantaneously conscientious {monitor your thoughts} you MUST be of the threat called DOUBT {ELOHIMS ENEMY -served on a platter}. My son, just as darkness and light can't occupy the same space in time; nor can Doubt and Faith occupy the same space in MIND! The mind is... the battleground!

The verb PULL; could be analogized for the Spiritual action of TRANSMUTATION! When you pull the trigger on the light switch, you instantaneously transmute a dark room into a lighted room. Therefore, when you squeeze the trigger of faith{SQUEEZE = BELIEVE: the substance of things hoped for; the evidence of things, not seen}before you doubt, you transmute the threat doubt would've caused and activate the LAW OF ATTRACTION to bring to you the desires you hoped for. It's much like Spiritual Martial Arts; using an adversary 's own momentum against them, unless you refer to it as majic!!.

Whether you believe it or not, the LIVING GOD is still active, and communicates with certain willful souls like yourself; youmayberejecting the right guidance and adhering to wrong voices, and maybe, that's why you keep attracting chaos; or not!. The data coming into your consciousness from the LIVING GOD, "IF" it's the Creator - LIVING GOD, presents the $64,000 question!, and... also the opportunity to commit the most heinous Spiritual crime{detrimental decision} in the Spirit World - **BLASPHEMY!**

Making the pivotal decision, whether or not it's GOD speaking, is where most people stumble. "HEARING VOICES ". They **are so afraid that somebody will judge them by the medical term "hearing voices ", not knowing they have the original gift Adam lost because of his**

93

.40 Cal: "Her nephew was killed with one; and she didn't like it !!

**DISOBEDIENCE, in the garden saga! He lost his ability {psychic} to-"see afar off": clairvoyant, clairaudient, etc. Hearing things that are inaudible, and seeing things that are invisible, truly qualifies as - afar off!**

**To be clear,** it's 'what' you believe about 'where' the information entering your consciousness is coming from that determines your level of faith, or doubt. If you keep doing the same thing and you get the same results; try something different, preferably the opposite.

Beware, you can get used to doing something wrong for so long, that doing that something correctly may feel like you are doing something wrong! Trust me son!

*[The boy seemed mesmerized at the changes Angelology has made in his Grand's life in only 5 years!]*

BLASPHEMY- is profanity; speaking offensively and sacrilegiously with regards to GOD about dramas you don't truly comprehend. If the voice is GOD'S and you believe it, it's considered faith by the Heavenly verdict. If the voice is GOD'S and you doubt it, well.., there'll be consequences for that decision also. Conversely, if the voice is SATAN'S and you believe it, you may have just signed a never ending contract of devolution, illusions, delusions, trials, misery, etc. If you want to steer clear of blasphemy, you need to know, you gain Favor from the Heavenly Host when you reject Satan's whispers. The angels taught him the truth about the spirit of rebellion; and NOW would be the best time to reject ELOHIM'S ENEMY - D-O-U-B-T!!

Please don't be confused about the speaking-hearing conflict. If you are hearing 'it' in your mind; SOME aspect of Y-O-U is speaking!

[As he gestures something that means- *there are many more dimensions to your soul than you comprehend]*

If you don't trust YOU, seek therapy!

If GOD speaks to you in HIS language, not yours: Whispers, Images, Sagas, Dramas, Dreams, Visions, Fables, Parables, Eagles, Foxes, books, babes, or winos; and you, unwittingly, proclaim the correspondences to be the DEVIL or anything other than GOD, and the images to be delusions; are you not profaning GOD?

**For example,** the court system convicted you to spend 100 years in prison, and you had a vision of being home on Thanksgiving of an unknown year, and you heard a small voice urging, "You are a Holy and Righteous God"; what would you accept, believe, or know to be true?

Then... if you, in the heartbeat of doubt and confusion, had the WISDOM to snatch that divine jewel from the whispers of the Heavenly Innerworld, **"You are a Holy and Righteous God",** and accept, believe, and down-right, just know, this was a message from the LIVING GOD, you WOULD TRANSMUTE the construct-ion of the template holding your dysfunction in place {literally break the chains} and activate the LAW OF

95

.40 Cal: "Her nephew was killed with one; and she didn't like it !!

ATTRACTION towards your higher, holy self. In other words my child, if you had reason to believe you were headed straight to hell when you died; you'd have just as much reason to believe you belong in Heaven, and you co-created by faith, a new BELIEF: " I'm going to be the EST angel in Heaven," for example. Thus, breaking the stronghold; you'll live to see ELOHIM'S Promise confirmed by deja vu,.. ONE - THANKSGIVING!!

On the other hand, if you don't know how to pull the trigger of faith, and you believe by (physical) sight and hearing, then that steel and concrete will be there for 100 years.

The noun TRIGGER; would therefore be analogized for the Spiritual WISDOM of - *KNOWING GOD HAS ALREADY DONE WHATEVER YOU DESIRED.*

As I said before, it's the adverb W-H-E-N, with its reference to Time, that makes all the difference in whether or not an aspirant's FAITH manifests their desires or not. W-H-E-N you are in the heartbeat of D-O-U-B-T is the ideal moment to **ACCEPT - GOD HAS ALREADY DONE** { *transmuted*} **WHATEVER YOU DOUBTED!** Then.. " Let go!!; let GOD, and .....WAIT!!"

So, to transduce this formula into bite sized morsels would mean- FAITH is best theurgized in the heartbeat of DOUBT." "Wowww!!, that's deep" Wiz said, nodding his head in agreement and walking away. It must've registered because, after he was about 15 feet away, he looked over his right shoulder at Popp, with a continuation of nods, and head-bobs, ".40 cal., huh?"

.40 Cal: "Her nephew was killed with one; and she didn't like it !!

*

Zing appeared impatient, and certainly with his newfound fame, didn't want to wait around for another one of the Sages' lectures. As far as Zing was concerned, his grandfather didn't understand how cool his friends were, despite constantly putting his neck on the line for them, and explaining why someone's behavior was below "THOROUGH" standards. He couldn't stand to hear Popp's lectures about jealous, so-called friends and their tell-tale signs either. So he pretended to act like it wasn't his turn by engaging in a phone call.

Padre noticed his anxiety and decided to approach him since he sensed his grandson wasn't coming to him; but before he did, he calculated the seconds it would take before his grandson would be in his presence. He decided 17 seconds wasn't enough Earth-time to bless his beloved progeny. So he had no choice but to morph into **milliseconds**, and afford himself 17,000 units of time to reach the Seventh Heaven, and supplicate to **EL ELYON**!

He pleaded, *"I AM seeking to solve a pervasive World problem involving the mentally, and spiritually enslaved. Your Arch-Rival has continued to mesmerize masses, like He did in the days of : JARED, ENOCH, METHUSELAH, LAMECH, and NOAH, including YOUR Elected 144,000.*

*Instead of using SORCERY - {pharmacopeia; chemicals; drugs}, CHARMS - {jewelry, fragrances, cosmetics} and ENCHANTMENTS - {music;*

.40 Cal: "Her nephew was killed with one; and she didn't like it !!

rhymes; hooks; spells} to lure Angels from their stations, He's created technological devices to imprison their souls and minds.

You promised me that each dissonating drama YOU would present before me should be viewed as a representation of 5,000,000 dissonating dramas occurring around the planet that STINK to HIGH HEAVEN! You elected and commissioned me to remember my boast and pray fervently for each situation as I deemed altruistic, and to exercise HOLY FAITH {Santa Fe} in believing, despite not being able to see 5,000,000 sagas, that as I pray for ONE, I will be praying fervently for ALL who suffer identical or similar scenarios!

You have NOT failed in your Covenant, nor shall I! So, as I come to the Seventh Heaven in Spirit, and I converse with YOU, MOST HIGH in Spirit, I will pray and exercise HOLY FAITH in Spirit, that you will allow **RAZIEL - {Keeper of the Secrets to the Mysteries of Heaven}** to provide a magical formula wherewith it may infuse into the population of mankind to spread like a pandemic towards the resolution of mankind's lack; including but not limited to: idol Worshiping, drug and alcohol dependency, immorality, avarice, sloth-complacency, hatred, two-faced falsehood, insolence, jealousy, and pride, etc. I'm supplicating, that for each virus YOU'D remove from the mind and soul of YOUR FAVORITE; YOU remove the same from my kinsman (LET MY PEOPLE GO!!!) the other 4, 999,999 souls. Also, replace the void with a virile mental construct viable for these current days and times to transmute the

98

advances of *YOUR ARCH-RIVAL; and for each soul that receives YOUR GIFT, YOU multiply their BLESSING 1,000,000 fold, and magnify their BLESSING 1,000,000 fold!* **As I LIVE and BREATHE, AMEN!!"**

The Wizard wrapped his proposal in Faith {*I AM the B-E-S-T World - problem solver there never was*}; left his request at the altar, and with lightning speed returned to *I.M.MORTAL PORTAL {wormhole}*; but this is the first time he had a new and exciting desire to infuse Earthlings with Jewells of the majic he was experiencing throughout these journals, since he invoked ELOHIM and HIS PRESENCE. Instantly! his RIGHT-HAND did a knee-jerk, or "hand-jerk reaction", and grabbed a handful of stars from the Galaxies he bypassed. His right-hand on Earth, however, balled up and clinched, and squoze into itself with Universal Power, like he had the world in his grasp.

Another millisecond later, His Astral joined its body on the terrace. He had 14,441 milliseconds left.

## Milliseconds

*The Milliseconds Covenant between Popp and ELOHIM began when the High Priest boasted to GOD that he (Popp) was going to be the first man to pray 1,000,000,000,000 {TRILLION } prayers before he died.*

*ELOHIM met this pomposity with hilarity and honor, and became cognizant of an energy exuding from HIS BEING that could only BE*

.40 Cal: "Her nephew was killed with one; and she didn't like it !!

described as a Covenant of Protection wrapping around the KINGS first tier generation of progeny.

When ELOHIM felt Impressed at Popp's Courage, HE assigned a myriad of Administrative Angels for daily assistance to be at his disposal as long as he remembers his own spoken covenant {boast} throughout his journey.

HE stationed a rack of Supernal Angels over his Archangels to ensure the Aspirant's Preceptors, and Administrative Angels wouldn't be misled or corrupted the way the WATCHERS were tempted and lured. ELOHIM wanted him to be given a fair enough chance to achieve his Spiritual aspirations without the totally unfair disadvantage of Shaitän and His minions. ELOHIM commissioned the supergiants (CHRONOS - linear Time) to expand or shrink TIME as the Theurgist needed, and HE commissioned (KAIROS - name means RIGHT MOMENT; coincidence, etc.) to synchronize TIME to harmonize his every concern related to his task.

ELOHIM liked the plans and preparation Popp invested in this supplication, and that initiative produced ADMIRATION for the co - creator, then ELOHIM envisioned his mind to have the BRILLIANCE of an

.40 Cal: "Her nephew was killed with one; and she didn't like it !!

Independence Day "Sparkler". In ELOHIM'S vision, Popp's mind twinkled like gold light on a chandelier.

ELOHIM asked Popp how he intended to do this... {telepathically of course}; and the answer had Angels rolling around on Heaven's floor laughing.

As well thought out as 50 Earth-years would allow, the Ascendant was prepared to meet his MAKER { die to self } and be the human/angel ELOHIM intended mankind to evolve into. As far as being prepared for the question, and being prepared for the task, he was indubitably, the hu-man for the job!!.

He began by explaining to the Creator of Heaven and Earth that if HE (ELOHIM) would allow him the GIFT to transmute each second into milliseconds, he (POPP) would tithe the first 100 milliseconds towards PRAISING and WORSHIPING.

{This caused ELOHIM to respect and exalt the WARRIOR}

"This way, I should stay covered by the blood that covers prayers, RIGHT?" he thought. It seemed only proper to Popp, If he was Praising,

.40 Cal: "Her nephew was killed with one; and she didn't like it !!

Worshiping, Tithing, and Transmuting, 60 times a minute, he should be covered by the Spirit eternally.

{ELOHIM chuckled mildly, while urging him to proceed}

He allocated another 100 milliseconds for THANKING and GIVING. " This", he thought, should surely please a GOD that constantly gives, and is rarely thanked.

{ELOHIM furled HIS brow in an unexpectedly curious expression, yet entertained more of POPP'S strategy. ELOHIM cast an undetectable ultraviolet light over POPP to literally see him in a different LIGHT}.

Popp dedicated another 100 milliseconds to GRACE and MERCY. Although he acknowledged his shortcoming when it came to FORGIVING, he felt like he'd visit the topic once a second at least, to see if he can make any necessary changes to his personality. He visited the limitations he had with people and drenched his adversaries with MERCIFUL BLESSINGS over their families, their finances, and their health.

{This melted ELOHIM'S heart to see the reflection in a man's heart for his fellow man. This caused some FAVOR to leak from his rib, and ooze out of

.40 Cal: "Her nephew was killed with one; and she didn't like it !!

HIS side in the spot where YESHUA was lanced. This FAVOR reached Earth and covered the entire city wherever Popp walked}.

WISDOM and UNDERSTANDING commanded their own respect and tenth of a second.

The Sage probably forgot the time he was a kid, sword-fighting with corrugated tubules, and a subtle voice whispered to him,"If you had 3 wishes;... just then, before the angel could finish, the young giant - slayer was raising his fake sword over his head to charge his adversary shouting, " I AM, the Courage of King David, AND the Wisdom of King Solomon, all at ONCE!!" HHUGHMPH!! As he thrust his imaginary blade into the air.

Only known to the Angel of Records {RADUERIEL}, the Courage and Wisdom were recorded in the Akasha as two of the three wishes.

So, he displayed extraordinary acuity at a young age.

They too, received 100 milliseconds of recognition for the reverence they deserve.

{ELOHIM felt the love in Popp as he EMBRACED the Wisdom GOD bestowed upon him. A BLESSING for Popp's success rose to the top of ELOHIM'S heart and struck at Popp like a Cobra}.

.40 Cal: "Her nephew was killed with one; and she didn't like it !!

*{ELOHIM assured Popp that HE too would help Popp become the first man on planet Earth to be credited with a trillion prayers. ELOHIM granted Popp a unique Wisdom to discern which sagas, dramas, occurrences, and ordeals are sent by GOD to test and enhance his triumphant challenge, as well as change the vibration on the planet; then HE granted him a level of UNDERSTANDING which seemed more like OVERSTANDING.}*

*{Popp knew UNDERSTANDING since he reached Earth. There've always been rumors about his childhood gifts and dreams, and then they stopped. One rumor: says the infant reached for his bottle; when the bottle didn't teleport, the infant blinked his eyes in expectation of retrieving it. The defeated baby-magi burst out into tears, quickly stopped, then tried again,..and again to teleport the desire by Attraction.}*

*The Covenant ELOHIM devised and Popp accepted was; "Each and every drama, incident, event, circumstance, accident, tragedy, or situation brought before Popp's life experience will be accounted as 5,000,000 prayers towards his: trillion prayer, self ascribed, extra curricular, soul redevelopment -* **PURPOSE!!!** *If and only IFFF Popp remembered to PRAY fervently for the souls depicted in the sagas!*

[Because ELOHIM'S creations manifest instantly, Popp was listening in silence to ELOHIM as HE was mixing a proverbial bowl of:

104

.40 Cal: "Her nephew was killed with one; and she didn't like it !!

GRACE x 5, STRENGTH x 7, LOVE x 9, to bestow into HIS Beloved's Planetary Auric Field to be received into Popp's 7 Chakras whenever his consciousness conceived the possibility of achieving the PURPOSE so eloquently designed.]

*Popp's Spirit leaked out a wonder whether or not the credit would account per saga or per individual. ELOHIM, of course, knows the multitude of gifts bestowed upon HIS fave; also picked up the scent of the wonder that leaked out, and responded to Popp's query with 5,000,000 per person.*

*The fifth portion of the milliseconds was left open for the appreciation of experiences, but first, the Wise-One wanted to make it as clear as possible what his part in the Covenant was, and exactly "WHAT" ELOHIM annnnnd HIS PRESENCE was committing to CONFIRM.*

*It could be extremely easy to make a prating fool of yourself claiming to have a Covenant with GOD.*

*The HUMAN/ANGEL reminded ELOHIM of his severe "TRUST/DISTRUST" issues and how defenseless he would feel to be taken advantage of by a "GIANT INVISIBLE BULLY"*

.40 Cal: "Her nephew was killed with one; and she didn't like it !!

*ELOHIM chuckled, but respected his honesty, then noticed a hiccup of CHARITY towards HIS ELECT. Next, ELOHIM agreed with HIMSELF that his hiccup was correct {as usual} and that HE should be more Charitable towards Popp's endeavors, after all, HE'S always wanted ONE man to take an interest in HIS Creation and its constituent members. As ELOHIM thought about the possibilities of having a WILLING soul to further HIS Original plan, it caused 8x measures of VICTORY, and 5x measures of INSPIRATION to ooze from the next exhalation of relief.*

*ELOHIM multiplied, then magnified, or magnified then multiplied the Holy Jewell's and stuffed them into the Chosen's auric field for transducing into neurological and electrical data, should any challenges of TRUST come before his Mighty; "Victorious-Conqueror", Soldier*

*The other half of the second was devoted to receiving messages back from the input he sent forth in the first half of the second.*

*This awesome influx of Spiritual Support empowered Popp to boast under his breath, so he thought, "The Lord won't have to come back to Earth, I'ma get this job - DONE!!"*

.40 Cal: "Her nephew was killed with one; and she didn't like it !!

*{ELOHIM smirked, and shook HIS head at the mortal's confidence, and tenacity. HE admitted to HIMSELF that HE fell in love with this hu-man.}*

When Popp acknowledged the convergence of his body and astral, he was squeezing the only item he had in his pocket.

He just knew, all the love he could summon in this admonishment, must have infused into this coin. Not yet realizing that his Higher-self grabbed a Universe of stars, and he was actually holding the world in his hands.

Now, he's realizing, his request was granted and he could bless his grandson and others.

Popp started by saying, "I thought you understood 'FORTUNE is wiser than FAME!!?"

Zing started to defend with his signature "I know!", when Popp abolished, "You must NOT!!" He took a breath, pressed the coin, walked in a circle and came back to eye-level when he asked him, "What the FUGCK, would make you INSTAGRAM $10,000 on your shoulder, or anything suggestive of it?"

He peered over his glasses and looked him in the eye. He took his glasses off, and looked him in the eye, and dared him to say 'sumpdin stupid," Popp was about to transform into Mr. Jekyll (STREET), and remembered to infuse "LOVE" into his coin. He was infuriated that O.G. had suggested a "MOCK" trunk-ride to scare some sense into him. His new hit song said," I been toting,.. Late-ly!!", so that may not have ended well!

.40 Cal: "Her nephew was killed with one; and she didn't like it !!

He was disheartened that the SON he elected to give his MANTLE; had his father's 'flashy' gene times 100, and he was perplexed to the highest PERPLEXITY as to WHYYY this boi keeps antagonizing all these haters!

Anyway!! STREET!! Would've been ready to take that coin and infuse it in Zing's eye, but POPP has had decades{aeons}of therapy. Besides, had the old "St." evoked, the poor boi wouldn't have seen it coming, nor would have understood the fury.

The grandfather may have maintained his composure, using antiquated therapeutic techniques, but intended to address his familial issues, using more modern, and spiritual techniques.

The Sage told his grandson, "I'ma pray about some things," and with a seldom look of disgust, began to turn his back on his child for all the times good Wisdom was disregarded, but said, "Wait" and handed him the coin.

This time he wasn't going to turn away. He watched his pro·té·gé, adorned in Worldliness, taking selfies as he heads for the terrace door.

"Heavy is the Head; that wears the CROWN," he thinks as the twilight star calls him to prayer.

At this shade of cerulean, he estimated the evening's end to be 12 minutes. He felt the gravity of this prayer was closer to a mourn than a praise and decided to wait a few minutes until dark. In the meantime, he'd find a bench, and enjoy the heavens. The stars seem to "TWINKLE" a li'l brighter around this color!, he thought! His eyes searched for his fave; the first Light;

108

the evening or morning star; Venus!! He enjoyed using the magnification of his eyeglass' lens to expand and contract the light around the star to form a "CRUX". For some reason, he took his glasses off to see what his myopia would reveal; and NO - MIRACLE, just some ole twinkling chandeliers.

When Zing and his impatience entered the elevator lobby, his first impulse was to take the 'stairs', but he unconsciously pressed the down button.

Something seemed 'ODD,' so he looked down to see the strange object slotted between his fingers. He "knee-jerk" scoffed, thinking, 'this is another trinket, magic charm that Popp would give out,' and shot a jump shot toward the cylindrical trash receptacle. The shot missed the trash receptacle, and 'dinged' when it bounced off the metal trash receptacle and rolled towards the track of the elevator's threshold. Zing left it there, and hurried to the ding of the DOWN elevator!!

In the "GLORIFIED" section of his mind, a voice was saying, "POPP didn't know I be bout dem ZEROS, not no shiny little trinkets," while he looked to the ceiling of the elevator to glimpse a reflection of himself.

As he exited the turnstile, a delivery truck blocked the driveway. The artistic owner painted; "PENNY FLOWERS," and drew a flower with a penny in the middle. The penny was shiny, and the artist chose to depict it- FACE DOWN!

When he got into the elevator of the garage, he again looked up to glimpse a reflection of himself; as he did, his grandfather who decided to pray

109

.40 Cal: "Her nephew was killed with one; and she didn't like it !!

into the darkness, was also 'LOOKING UP', but for a different reason, ....to a different - GOD!!

The Master Theurgist was all alone on the grand terrace, and needed to 'SIGN-IN' to his "GOD ACCOUNT.

He spoke towards the evening star and said;

*I.M. Mortal Portal, you won't recognize M.E.*
*Not my wheels, as they turn; not my soul, Astral free!*

*I.M. Mortal Portal, veiled dimensions, will I peep;*
*I have Visions when awake; Lucid dreams, when asleep!*

*I.M. Mortal Portal, DARK as MATTER, "LIFE of TREE;"*
*'KASHIC RECORDS, Seventh Heavens, distant places, Yeah,.. I BE!!*

*I.M. Mortal Portal, ears won't fathom, eyes can't see; but if you ask...then*
*I'll share what ARC GABE reveals to M.E.*
*[#777]*

He closed his mouth and opened his mind, to hear the cadence of his prayer, floating across the quiet stillness of the heavens. He didn't hum or chant anything after his prayer, he just listened, and breathed 9 cycles, or at least tried to!! Then his body felt a reverberating jolt!, ...more like a VOLT!

He knew the gates to the vault had been opened! As Yeshua said, "Someone touched Me, for I knew it when power went out from Me"; and from here on out, it will be "From his lips to God's ears."

Popp believed he was favored by God, because of his unselfishness in prayer. The way he asked GOD to Bless: the Earth, Moon, stars, angels, animals, forestry, and all the way back to every soul he's ever witnessed since grade school;...he was RIGHT!!

Tonight's prayer will bypass the usual, and get straight to the family issues!

He prayed for every possible human complaint and complainer that he'd witnessed during his sojourn, and magnified each blessing for each woe times a million and justified this as the greater good for mankind.

Then he started sending faithful energies to the members of his family; beginning with the oldest senior.

He rested his loving, protecting, teaching energies on the absolute youngest; the first link to a whole new generation; the one we ALL have gathered for;... his first great grandson!!!

He stilled his mind, and asked with his heart; if the Creator of Heaven and Earth could feel the electricity he was possessing in his heart. Then, from the depths of the deepest stillness, he heard...

.40 Cal: "Her nephew was killed with one; and she didn't like it !!

*MIGHTY STAR!, so powerful you are,*
*Won't lose your connections from afar,*

*Born and destined to BE who you are!*
*O Mighty Star! O Mighty Star!*

*May the Rivers of Strength flow through you;*
*As God protects you, and the things you do!*

*No dams, nor walls, will block your flow*
*COME DOWN!! strong-holds, everywhere, you go!*
*[#555]*

As soon as he noticed the downpour of blessings coming from the SOURCE of all Creation; he began deflecting his might towards the unborn and his father like a constant flow of Sun rays bouncing off the mirror. He made use of the abundant love by blessing neighbors and others, and even included their loved ones.

A light bulb went off in his head that a McDonald's sandwich was in the backpack which Wizzard took to the room!!

.40 Cal: "Her nephew was killed with one; and she didn't like it !!

[*He tries as best as he can to respond to the picture-languages as expediently {OBEDIENCE} as possible. He knows the only Secret to Obedience that was never revealed. You never know when you're entertaining an angel.*]

Despite loving his new job - Walking with ELOHIM, he'd break prayer for an unassociatable pop-in message. He wasn't exactly hungry, but he'd been there all day and was ready to leave. Except!!...He had to go back to the room.

Back at the room, Myesha was stressed out and knocked out. Wiz went back to the "BREAD & MEAT." He couldn't fathom, missing an opportunity to profit, nor could he forgive, allowing a customer to get away.

Popp assured everyone he would be back tomorrow and hand gestured a joke to Nanna, to look at the clock; it was 11:59 pm. She caught the joke late when it became midnight; she was tired too!

The expecting paternal grandmother didn't usually answer her phone in the wee hours of the morning, however, she thought, as well as hoped, someone would be telling her that her first grandchild was here. Instead... a frantic caller, from an unknown number, was screaming, what sounded like, "Your son's been shot!   She tried and tried to get clarity over the calamity, but all she heard before the 'click-up", was background noise and shuffling. Eventually, the unknown number never responded again.

# 4th QUARTER

Work Smart-est; .. from the Hearts!

Play Heart-est;... it Stops, as Starts!

**The phone rang! But Popp refused to answer it. He'd just fallen on the motel bed, and hadn't dared to journal, shower, nor put anything away. It had been a beautifully eventful day...**

[*The first SIGN he absolutely, positively KNEW, early this morning, that the day was going to be fantabulous, was the light from the Sun refracted off the mirror in the bedroom and shone a beam of light on a unique displacement of gel inside the sclera of his eye, once it was open, that made the teeny irritant glisten like a diamond; but his intra- periphery observed what appeared to him as a chandelier twinkling in the moving sunlight!, right inside the orbit of his iris!!*

*Next: he started to pray the Lord's Prayer over Rose as he did every morning, and she began to recite in unison even with her eyes closed. Then she opened them, and stated in her sultry morning voice, "Your skin appears to have a beautiful violet undertone with those sun rays beaming on your dark handsome face,..making your birthmark glow honey!!", as she blessed him with a morning kiss!! He made a mental note that the Harmony was remarkable, as well as the kiss.*

*When he went through the kitchen to put the dog outback, he noticed the microwave light flashing. So when he came back in he washed his hands and opened the microwave door; SURPRISED!! to see the cup of coffee he never drank from yesterday! All he had to do was push the button!!*

### The PRESENCE of ELOHIM is relentless in REVELATIONS.

*So IT continued: he went to turn on the water for the shower; someone inadvertently left the shower governor open to the perfect pressure, and whatever the angels did with his hands, it was the perfect temperature!*

*Then, even though they weren't running late or anything this morning, the very first parking space was available in the Long-Term parking lot at the airport.*

*So consequently, he'd been journaling the Lord's PRESENCE all day!*]

In his exhaustion, he was most appreciative to have been Elected to walk with the LIVING GOD! Though it's NOT the easiest job, it certainly has the greatest fringe benefits!

The last 5 years in Angelology have produced exceptional: mysteries, relations, paradigms, coincidences, perceptions, deductions, skills, interests, and abilities in a person whose trajectory was either death or prison by the age of 25.

He was truly grateful for how his life, and the lives of family and friend's changed because of ELOHIM'S guidance. His changes and prayers inspired some people,

[*no one in the BOOK of LIFE: caught COVID or lost their jobs*]

and he was using every ounce of: Love, Honor, Respect, Gratitude, etc. to praise ELOHIM, the MOST HIGH {EL ELYON}, and SOURCE {INEFFABLE}while he laid across the bed like a CRUX!!

He was so ineffably overjoyed with the way his physical self felt, as it merged with his High-est Spiritual self, and the twain merged with SOURCE, that he wanted to maintain the CURRENT feelings for an Entity for an Eternity!!! He didn't read anything else into it! He attributed: the prayers, the moon, the stars, the mountains, the Falls, the travel, the State, the upcoming Equinox, and everything except the Power of his Divinity-Pedigree!!Obedience, Love, Patience, Understanding, or Faith for the Miraculous experience he was having in the Southwest!

***SAINT*** - as he is *currently referred to in Psychic Circles; is literally-spiritually 'PLUGGED-IN'!!*

.40 Cal: "Her nephew was killed with one; and she didn't like it !!

His relationship with ELOHIM blossomed. He was insatiable about the feeling, like he was plugged into the Sun, and didn't want THAT sensation to ever leave, nor fade, nor disappear into the recesses of his subconscious mind; plus he just laid atop BOCA NEGRA - volcanic mountain, and didn't want THAT energy to fade either! The emerging energies caused a physical sensation he never ever experienced!! . He felt like the SUN had indwelled his WHOLE- HEART, so he did what any RIGHTEOUS MAGI would do, and used one of the Ancient Devotions taught by KAIROS to let GOD know he was grateful, and pleased with his present situation; unlike most humans who bicker and complain about theirs! 'Angels HATE that', he thought!

He tuned into the rhythm of his BREATHING, which he now knows is another Angelic GIFT, [RAZIEL taught him 'EVE' translates to *'BREATH OF LIFE'!!]*

After being Elected to be an Angelologist, *{actually the MECHANICOLOGY to the 144,000}* his Metaphysical perceptibility grew exponentially, and when your paradigm changes exponentially, YOU change exponentially!! and he was certainly enjoying life's changes, and almost refused to believe that a changed paradigm would create such a wonderful new world!!

He was Favored amongst angels and they taught him things 'ears won't fathom; eyes can't see!!'

Even in his somnambulism, you could detect his understandable disdain for mankind's irreverence towards the etherworld, as he scoffs thinking, 'they'll literally forget Mother Eve's contribution to LIFE, also.'

He decided to switch into meditative mode, because he realized his disdain for mankind's irreverence towards ELOHIM'S Mercy was causing tension in his body. He lucidly flipped over, still shaped like a cross, but still maintained his spiritual connection from afar, and kept his place in line at Spiritland while his lucidity kicked off his shoes.

He began the lucid meditation by slowing his breathing. Then he gradually deepened the inhalations while affirming, "As I live and breathe," nine times!!; and slowly extended the exhalations, while affirming "As YOU live, I breathe "

After a few cycles of his chest raising up and down, he was ready to do the magic of devotions and secure his BLISS on Earth. He had no remorse whatsoever, that no one else that he knew, had been taught these Secrets and Laws at an early age, and he was in no hurry to give these secrets away.

He monitored two more deep breathing cycles to make sure he wasn't inhaling too deeply nor extending the exhale too much. His goal was to pace his breaths, like a runner, to ensure the stamina of the 9-cycle praise.

*[He would inhale with the INTENT to REFLECT to ELOHIM the present situation; his exhale would, as B-est he could, INTEND to ENVISION*

118

.40 Cal: "Her nephew was killed with one; and she didn't like it !!

*(Hear,See) GOD'S solution back out into the world; leave it at the Altar, and be paced for the next inhalation!!]*

*The paced chant would go like this:*

*"As I live and breathe;*
*As YOU live, I breathe "*

*N*ext, he summoned the Supernal Angel CHRONOS for anything - ETERNAL, and he was putting in a request to maintain this level of connectivity with SOURCE, Forever!!. Being a trillion years old, others refer to this Angel as ANCIENT of DAYS! Popp never told anyone he had a personal relationship with FATHER-TIME!!!

He started to *flashb...*

*After Popp left Liza on New Year's day; his very first prayer that year was quite impactful. He swore to GOD, because he hadn't been Presenced to ELOHIM yet.*

*He promised he would never ever fix his lips to say the 7 YEARS with Liza were a waste of time. The more meaningful portion of the prayer was denouncing the clichés of wizardry, "That was a waste of time."*

.40 Cal: "Her nephew was killed with one; and she didn't like it !!

*He "pulled the trigger" at that pivotal juncture, and what he co-created with GOD was: "I Thank you Father for the opportunity to invest the TIME you allowed into your Holy daughter , if YOU felt the need, YOU would certainly grant me 7 more years, I'd hope".*

*He heard, in the distant subtleness, "You will receive 77 years!" He pulled that trigger and added 77 to 50 and scoffed, [*an 'Act of Faith'- scoff!!] *"I better start an exercise program!"*

A millisecond later:

He acknowledged Father Time in as many aspects as he could: "Thanks for the day I was born; Thanks when I thought I was late, and avoided an accident; Thanks it never rains on us, then we hear rain drops after we enter shelter, etc."

Then he began to reconnect with all the altruistic energies that he intended to be in his daily life.

When his paradigm reconnected to the CURRENT energy, he turned off words, and mental transmissions to beseech with his whole heart, that this is the way he enjoyed his life proceeding and he wanted ELOHIM to feel his current situation and know he of all humans, was grateful for the air he breathed, and  through his breath, he wanted to "Give Thanks." So, while he was tethering righteous vibrations, he began to cycle that bliss - 9 times!!

At the mental stamina's end, at the completion of the 9th cycle, his meditation crossed into dream world. The first dream was a collage of this day's travel graces: the skies were serene; the landing-smooth!, the milkshake at Route 66 ⟨ROUTE⟩ **66** was - NICE!; the falls at the Pueblo Reservation were phenomenal; climbing the volcanic mountain was breathtaking! And his new travel partner was Gracious2b!!

The second dream had 5 year segments of the kids' lives! Each ministry featured dramas, sagas, or events in each of the kids' lives. One 5 year segment reflected the night or morning Wiz was grazed on the same day his first son was born.

The next dream or vision zoomed in on Rose, getting out of the shower and bringing him the phone!

Just then, he was superconscious of being in the motel and even heard the bathroom door open. Thereafter, the phone on the desk rang. In one smooth grab, Rose had the towel in her left hand and scooped the phone with her right.

Popp opened his eyes to see her handing him the phone.

He didn't acknowledge the caller ID, nor would he have known the foreign number. Amidst the background noise and sirens, he could barely make out someone repeating "Popp," through the numerous interruptions.

.40 Cal: "Her nephew was killed with one; and she didn't like it !!

Another call emerged and the ID was S.I.L.; he quickly answered his {son in law} and said, "Wassup DINK?"

Dink stammered a bit before he said, "Popp...I think your grandson's been shot!!" Thinking that God's protecting Grace had saved Wiz 4 times, he took for granted he would survive the 5th! Even though Popp was 2,000 miles away, he still asked Dink, "Where is he?"

Dink hesitatingly said, "COLFIELD." Instantly...Popp knew this wasn't Wiz, it must be ZINGG!! He told Dink he'd call him back, and hung up! He called DUCHESS who was like a mom to ZING and lived near the incident.

She confirmed it was a Silver Coupe! Nobody could be sure through the deeply tinted windows, but a body was slumped over the steering wheel, and a diamond studded cross was refracting off the dashboard. He thanked her and called S.I.L.

"It's ZING," he told his daughter's husband, who'd been the fatherly point of contact throughout the young man's life. Dink was in denial about his stepson and the 20 years invested into him.

Popp wasn't scheduled to return to the East Coast for 18 days! and no one in his family would dare discuss street issues on the phone. Despite his new growth and direction, it was just C-O-D-E, and it would be a while before he could freely discuss whatever happened to his Sun.

.40 Cal: "Her nephew was killed with one; and she didn't like it !!

SAINT didn't allow the news to steal his Joy. Therapy, and the angels taught him how to regulate the highs and lows of what is now considered to be Bi-polar disorder{*formerly Manic Depressive Psychosis; Neurosis*}.

It was quite peculiar, from his unique and spiritual aspect, that his grandson's life was returned to its Creator on the evening he settled into Santa Fe, New Mexico.

He never "Questions" ELOHIM'S ways, per se, even though ELOHIM keeps him knowing, deducing, conjecturing, and theosophizing on GOD'S ways and mysteries!

He didn't have the words to speak to his daughter yet, nor would she be answering the phone for the next few days. So he, too, turned off his phone and began to write. This is what he posted on her Facebook page:

*Grandson...listen to me, this is ALL my fault.*

*The tragedies that occur in BALTIMORE CITY are blood on MY HANDS.*

*When you were young and YOUR father Winston was locked up and I didn't STEP-UP & STEP-IN for you and others like you, who had fathers that were incarcerated, I left a VOID in your SOUL that nothing else but a REAL-MAN could fill.*

.40 Cal: "Her nephew was killed with one; and she didn't like it !!

When I was SELFISH with my TIME, and invested only in my personal pleasures and NEGLECTED to invest in your future, I blindly caused you to SEEK GUIDANCE amongst your peers.

When I told you "Be Careful. ...JEALOUSLY is MURDER; ENVY is a SHOVEL, and a SMILE could be a BULLET ", I didn't explain how I was your KILLER.

You SEE,...EVERY TIME I compliment the FRESH PAIR on your feet, a BULLET releases from my HEART.

When I EVIL-EYE you because of your beautiful GIRL, and the ENVY causes me to want to be in your fresh pair of shoes, a bullet releases from my heart.

When **GREED** consumes me, and I believe if you get paid, that somehow keeps me from getting paid, another bullet I've fired at you.

When my **SLOTH** ( laziness ) satisfies me, and you're ON YOUR GRIND, a big blast is released from that SHOTGUN deep down in the depths of my soul.

When the **FALSEHOOD** in my smile covers the motive that I'm only ROLLING with you to CLOCK your MOVES, I'm slicing your carotid artery with a razor blade each time you let me get behind you.

.40 Cal: "Her nephew was killed with one; and she didn't like it !!

*Because my **PRIDE** ( however FOOLISH ), won't allow: public debasement; a loss (which is part of the game ); another man recognizing the beautiful woman I'm also neglecting; being called a LABEL I've clearly demonstrated that fits me, it TRIGGERS my **WRATH** (anger) and my mind won't reason and ALL I obsess about is the many ways to KILL YOU.*

*When I examine my SOUL to make sense of my ways, I  discover that the **LUST** for POWER I desire to have, is an indelible imprint on the formation of my soul from the time of KINGS when I was Great and Respected, and Rich, and Powerful, and blew it ALL because of my: PRIDE, GREED, ENVY, SLOTH, ANGER, and FALSEHOOD.*

*Then my SHAME rose up and I contemplated SUICIDE, and in my DISTORTION I looked in the mirror, but the mirror was YOU, cause you look like M.E.! So my distortion transformed into a DELUSION now that I'm DRUGGING and I panicked, because I'm about to be discovered that I've been a BITCH of a MAN. Then I reached for my GUN to try to kill the TRUTH, so I aimed at the shame that I saw in the mirror, and I pointed at my chest, in a split second later a few POUNDS on the trigger released ALLL my HATE for SELF when the bullet entered YOU!!*

*BALTIMORE…my grandson ( SELFMADE-ZING ) This is ALLL my fault.*

.40 Cal: "Her nephew was killed with one; and she didn't like it !!

*So I apologize to your mother Myona, and all the other mothers who have SONS that I have murdered. I apologize to aunts, uncles, grandparents, sisters, brothers, and many many cousins that I have left empty-hearted.*

*PLEASE PLEASE FORGIVE ME,*

*POPP!*

\*

Meanwhile, back East; rumors, theories, and speculations abound through the gossip circuits.

There were theories: that he was retaliated against because of his brother, and that he was shot with a .40 Cal; the religious folks felt God needed an Angel; one of the east sider's brothers who was killed during the massacre when ZING's dirt bike was involved, was also amongst the suspects.

You also had rumors of a scorned witch brewing against his grandfather; a scorned older woman, for denying her baby, had her brother involved; the nemesis of his younger cousin BARK, for intervening in an induction ceremony, and the list goes on and on!

The speculations involved: he fired on someone and his gun jammed, theirs didn't; he wanted to be like his brother, and wasn't; the GOOD, die young!; he got what he deserved, blah, blah, blah!!! There was so much mayhem behind: who, what, when, where, why and how?!, that innocent persons names were introduced into the saga.

Zing's true homies started their own campaign to find out what happened to their comrade... FORCE!!!

One segment of the family wanted the law to handle the situation; the other side didn't want any police involvement whatsoever.

Even Zing's mother had reservations about who would be leading the investigation. At the vigil, one detective approached her and asked, "Miss...do you know whether or not your son owned a .40 Cal?" Overwhelmed with emotion she responded, "What?..what are you saying?..My son was shot with a .40 Cal?" The detective had no headway with the hysteria, so he said, "Miss...do you want us to find your son's killer, or not?" What did he say that for? Her tears instantly stopped; she handed her husband her quickbag; she pushed her sleeves up her forearm; walked towards him and said, [*pointing that index finger at his comprehension*] "As a matter of fact, I don't want YOU to do NOTHING for my son!!. Aren't you the one whose partner was mysteriously murdered in an alley down at the PITS? Huh!! Find YOUR partner's murderer! Do that!" as she side glanced to let him know there were plenty of rumors about his practices floating around the streets, including, 'he shot Wiz'. Then she closed her brief interview, walking away saying, "Then you can worry about my son's killer after you find your partners." Her face was red, and her nose was flared.

.40 Cal: "Her nephew was killed with one; and she didn't like it !!


Being the smartass detective he was known to be, he surrendered his hands and with smug sarcasm asked, "Are you sure?"

With her back turned, she threw up DEUCES, and whispered, in her sweet, harsh voice, "Don't worry, my family takes care of their own!"

Then she angrily started reciting a revision ZING made of Popp's creed; *[even though the kin didn't think she knew it]* again she thought she was speaking softly, but she soon realized she had a following when she whispered,


"We don't play, in these fucking streets;

You fucks wit us, we brings dat HEAT!"

First, one millennial walking behind her repeated it, then, another and another. Next, people who didn't even know what they were saying; were chanting and following the crowd that gathered.

No one knew, the three kin used ZING's revised version of Popp's creed to forge their street pact. When Zing was cutting his teeth in the rap game, he would often remake or sample various familiar beats and practice his freestyling on his kin. So one day, he kept Wiz and Cherokee, rolling on the floor laughing as he sampled various remakes of Popp's creed. It became the oath to their bond; they even shared bloodletting.

*

.40 Cal: "Her nephew was killed with one; and she didn't like it !!

**Zing's female cousins and other millennials had one thing on their minds - REVENGE!!** Whatever it was about the handsome, debonair, young entrepreneur, it sure pissed his contemporaries off, that some hater ended his life!

*

The true comrades had a different technique...FORCE! They were literally leaning on people for info! They were snatching people into trunks, vans, and alleys! One interrogator -BLEED! - had remarkable ways of extracting information. There are way too many stories about how he got his name! Needless to say, it probably had something to do with - BLOOD!

*

Myesha was another wounded soul from the tragedy. She paced back and forth across the kitchen floor; either talking to herself, or cursing out ZING! She was saying "Boi...you make me sick! That's why I can't stand yo ass...cause you do dumbass shit like this. What the fuck were you thinking? You had it made man!! I can't fucking stand you dumbass, etc." Just out of General Principal, she too, wanted to avenge her brother-in-law.

*

.40 Cal: "Her nephew was killed with one; and she didn't like it !!

His own mother's heart was evacuated in his absence. It was the biggest shock of her entire life. Especially since he was considered the "GOOD" son. She often reflected on the ole saying "the GOOD die YOUNG," to get her through the day.

At gang headquarters, a different kind of growth is upon us; more like cancer on steroids!! The TEACHER has his own idea of the kind of Creative Craft he'll be teaching. He actually believes he should start a college of sorts; what exactly are you teaching a woman, 9 months pregnant, by kicking her down a flight of stairs?; and how exactly did you acquire your grandfather's Jewells in the *"BOOK of LIFE"?* Huh!!?

Wiz (I'm sorry, TEACHER of Jewells: he titled himself ) had them recite the original creed in the morning  hustling ceremonies, but the  revised version in the  mourning  ceremonies, before the .40 Cals. go ablazing!! Sometimes he'd teach them a light poem; nothing majical, unless they had the rank. He taught certain poems, odes, prayers, and spells, depending on his ranking system. Then he taught the revised Jewells to the nightshift, and to others with certain status; at that meeting is where he taught esoteric Jewells. He even wrote his own Jewell and told his crew to harmonize it if anyone felt like someone bewitched them or their family.

.40 Cal: "Her nephew was killed with one; and she didn't like it !!

*A Mountain's Curse*
   *in oathen days!?*
*Blaspheme, I say,*
   *blaspheming ways!?*
*I should not swear,*
   *but could not Praise!?*
*Cast threads with,*
   *backwards Fingers Braze!?*

*Lest Wise reveal,*
   *the Strands of Craze!?*
*Hang Upside down,*
   *in Weaver's Maze!!!!*

Teach had an entire staff meeting where he instructed 25 underlings to keep their ear to the street. He told them to report any clue they heard directly to him. No rumor was too small! He wanted every bit of information there was pertaining to the death of his brother. Then he pointed to the back door and said, "Why are yall still here?"

After the crew jumped from the chairs and bottle necked the back door, Teach gave the eye to the inner circle of look-alikes to stay behind, he felt something odd and wanted to show them a technique!

His phone rang and whoever was on the other end must've revealed something because he told Carrot to call back 3 of the minions while he was still conversing. Carrot whistled out the bottleneck and put up 3 fingers. Since Teach rewarded initiative, there was never a shortage of volunteers; three day-ones looked at each other in a split decision and hauled ass back to headquarters. Each was probably thinking about the 5k each earned on the last job!

He reminded his DAY-ONE'S how important LOYALTY was to him and sent them to kill his 16 year old cousin.They all turned and ran towards the bottleneck; Li'l Woosy reached out his hand to touch the door when he reached it first. He immediately turned around and dashed with even more speed towards the bosses' peering eyes, as they watched him run towards them with two outstretched fingers indicating he won both races!! Despite Bossman listening to his informant, he reached in his pocket and pulled out two 5 dollar bills, gave them to Woosy and continued listening.

In the darkroom meeting, he reassured the inners of his promise to portions of the insurance money when it arrived, but first he felt some eeriness.

He stood atop the unknown sigil inside the 9 pointed figure inside the 9 ft. diameter circle. He had the crew hold hands, left-over-right, around the circle! Their job was to recite the chants, while he, being unusually theatrical, recited his Jewells. He held some gem that usually rested on the pedestal next to the *BOOK of LIFE.* Then he started his recitation of some adulterated and distorted versions of some chants and spells, because he felt some eeriness trying to entangle him.

*[He envisioned 2 hands dripping candle wax, afar off, downward onto a downward facing penny]*

After the brief ceremony was over, he signaled to someone to blow out the candles and proceeded to the upper room.

After the alcoholic feast, he assuaged their conscience by telling them it had to be done!

*[And takes a bite from his favorite apple- Delicious]*

He reiterated to the crew that the outfits he coordinated on the last heist had items out of Zing's GOOD WILL donations; the only evidence that could harm his crew was a knit hat that fell off at the scene. The scully and DNA belonged to ZING, and Teach knew Zing wasn't going to prison for any of his grimy shit.

He gave his team an entire playbook on how to scatter various rumors throughout the city!

On the 'West siiide!', he spread rumors that he was looking for guys from the 'East siiide!"

In Cherry Hill he asked his little cousin when was the last time he saw Zing and who was the older woman in the rumors, that was sure to get her brother's gang on alert!

When he spoke with the leader of the 33rd St. gang, he asked if their sister-gang pillow-talked any information out of the Eastside crew about his brother's death. This certainly turned the Upper East against the Lower East,

He assured the family that the streets 'would take care of their own.' He took the axiom to new levels with a different interpretation of this maxim than his grandfather taught!

*

Aside from Zing's fiancee Dominique, no female felt  more violated or heartbroken than his aunt. ***SILHOUETTE*** - as she is referred to now, felt like the jewel of her heart had been taken. She too, has changed exponentially in 5 or so years!

.40 Cal: "Her nephew was killed with one; and she didn't like it !!

[*It appears she has taken on her Father's Mantle; you can expect phenomenal occurrences wherever she goes also, but she hasn't yet attributed these coincidences to anyone or anything in particular, especially not her pedigree or angels! In her patrilineal pedigree, she is triple blessed with psychic abilities: Numerology, Onomatology, and Angelology! We'll see how these gifts unfold!*]

The males in the Righteous bloodline display attributes of their newfound gifts at age 18, but it hasn't been revealed when the females receive their endowment. She's left-handed, so does that make her receive her endowment when the males receive theirs? Perhaps, but it sure looks like SILHOUETTE is going to be at least 3 times more powerful than her father; just as he prophesied. Even her simplest utterances come True; whether it be a joke or sarcasm, whatever she mentions comes True!

She credited ZING as the impetus, as well as, catalyst to her Fashion success; because he prophesied that she would be successful and pointed out to her, all the prophecies which came True for him. Her high-fashion catsuit company had blown up and taken the world by storm, and she looked forward to the day she could fly him in her private jet; the one they'd fantasize about when they'd sit on the back of the truck after flea market on Saturdays watching the planes as they landed at the private airport in Linthicum. She wanted to remind him of another childhood prophecy and bring him to see her penthouse in Dubai.

She had the resources and connections to find out who killed her nephew, but apprehension gripped her, because deep down in her ultra-professional soul, she desired to personally handle her family's affairs with poetic justice and leave the 'sonofaBITCH' in the same chalk line her nephew laid in!

She even thought about the McDonald's bag her father placed in her sock drawer at her townhouse in the city. She was about to go ballistic; thinking her father put food in her drawer until she opened the bag to find a brand new, never fired, .40 Cal, and some spare keys to Zing's garage and bikes. She could barely believe the coincidences, but she's the baby-girl and knew coincidences were the first-signs of GOD'S PRESENCE that she best not ignore!!

She even reflected on a sermon Popp gave to Wiz about the difference between; DEATH ANGELS, and ANGELS OF DEATH!! He assured Wizzard that if GOD'S enemy is Divinely delivered into your hands, you're an A.O.D. If you go out seeking to kill you're the other.

Silhouette thought about the special design catsuit she created for Myesha to secure all her weapons of the craft. All she had to do to turn it into the perfect hit-woman attire was to turn the pouches inward, aback a waist trainer type fabric.

She thought often about avenging her nephew's death but dare not go out seeking. It was like Zing kept chanting their oath in her mind. He'd become bitter and mischievous on the other side.

Her plane was about to land, and she wanted to say a prayer to ensure whichever path elected, would be RIGHTLY GUIDED!

Tears came to her eyes while she *reminis….*

*"Dawter, if you ever want a Prayer that is 1,111,111.11% guaranteed to Amaze you'll be walking with the LIVING GOD,  say this one "*

The prayer was named - **RASHID!**

> *My lips work!; to whom shall I babble?*
> *My arms work!; who shall I embrace?*
> *My feet work!; which way shall I travel?*
> *My smile works!; if they shall see Your FACE!!*
> *[#111]*

She let the essence of those words resonate inside the quietude of her mind, as she breathed the enchantments for 9 cycles!

The confirmation came as she was walking through the airport. Light refracted off some object, 200 feet up the corridor. She couldn't make out what it was because it sparkled briefly, and her movement assured she wouldn't be in that exact spot again!

She needed to find a restroom to change into her BS3's and shed the European attire. She received multiple compliments on her Copper Edition Catsuit. Perhaps it was the paradigm of copper that allowed her to capture the sparkle of a penny resting in the doorway of the women's restroom. What was so unique and supernatural about the penny was; it wasn't on heads nor tails, it was standing up, or darn near standing up against the wall. It appeared to be rolling and stopped in the track of the threshold. The track had a slot that allowed the security curtain to slide through, and the penny fit much like a tire in a pothole. The most peculiar aspect of the find was; the face on the penny that was standing at 15° was perfectly aligned in the upright position. Even more paranormal was, at first glance, she saw her nephew's face in the bust's head on the penny. She reached down and picked the coin up by its side because it wasn't laying flat. When she washed her hands, she washed the penny and sat it on the back of the sink. She pulled out her quick bag that kept her BS3's, then she unzipped her catsuit and turned it inside out. She rolled it up and put it in the quick bag. She put on the black shirt-hoodie; then the black slacks-sweatpants, and the black sneakers- Nike. She dried the penny, put it in her pocket, grabbed her stuff and split!

The funeral's tomorrow and the women in the family would meet at Myona's Hair Salon; another ZING production. Not only was Zing's mom a great hair stylist, she did the best POCAHONTAS French Braids; the two braids that hung down the sides of the women's faces. The braids accentuate the widows peak and bring out the features of their CHEROKEE heritage. You could always tell Popp's girls at a function.

Zing's other aunt-TANEKA-was in her BS3's and on her NINJA cycle to attend the all female version of the family meeting. This ONE right here y'all...whew!! "Ain't nothing to play with!" Been riding the bike and banging IYON since she was 9 years old, sharp shooter too! Black Belt at 14; government trained and was a ROLLIE when POPP was STREET and the creed was "Bring me the HEAD, send the body to the Mama!" She threw her hair in a SISTERHOOD ponytail and headed outside the Pennsylvania line.

Zing's other aunts would attend the meeting, but they thought all that dressing alike was corny. One meeting, SHAWNEE was joking with Taneka when Taneka explained it wasn't planned. The family discovered over numerous, random encounters, that when one member wore a black shirt, black slacks, and black sneakers, as many as 7 other members wore BS3's. This happened on various occasions, at numerous places, and none were funerals. For this,.. ZING'S homegoing, it will be intentional!! So Shawnee, Dana, Robin, and ROYCE agreed to suit-up their BS3's in honor of ZING. Wiz took it to another level, he and all the look-alikes wore BS3's all the time,..even in the summer!

.40 Cal: "Her nephew was killed with one; and she didn't like it !!

*

At Myona's, all the clients were finished and the girls took the meeting into the basement lounge.

Myona invited 4 of her stylists to attend. This was unusual, but strategic. Each stylist represented one of the cardinal directions of the city, and was sure to be a wealth of information. Their collective clients would bring rumors and gossip from north, south, east and west of Midtown.

One of the stylist -TABRISHA-was Bleed's sister. She overheard him telling a soldier to investigate the rumor that a look-alike in BS3's was shooting craps in the Colfield area around sundown that day! There was no need for any of Wizzard's people to be working that area; that wasn't how they agreed to split up the territories.

A bright light went off in Silhouette's head when she heard that report. She started putting various parts of the puzzle together and deduced that Wiz built his empire using family rules and practices, some of which he'd take too far! She believes now that his gang is his family he may have divulged the secret of the Twilight Star, and other family jewells!

Myona was infuriated at the thought that her seed was so ruthless, to not only consider it, but to have his brother murdered; and began ranting, "I believe it!!I feel it!! I believe that shit...that sick, psychotic motherfucker is so fucking ruthless, he might even have me kilt! The fucking psycho" and on and on!

Taneka thwarted the rant when she asked, "Does anybody have any idea which look-alike it was shooting dice?"

One of the millennial cousins said, "TOOK...is the cute one!"

Another cousin said, "Don't they all look alike! Ain't that why they call them look-alikes?" The first gawked, "They DO...all look-alike, but his widow's peak is deeper, and his eyebrows are thicker!" Myona responded, "You see that? That's what I'm talking about! The cruddy bastard is so smart, he even recruited a team of thugs that look-alike, all to confuse authorities." The women consoled her, but couldn't comfort her.

They concluded the meeting and agreed to meet at the viewing.

Silhouette was the first to arrive. She believed "To be early, is to be on-time; to be on-time, is to be late!" She stood alone over her nephew. Of course propounding life without him. She appreciated his mother dressing him in his BS3's. He preferred to swag his black sneakers with patent leather striped Adidas! His hair was always tight. His widow's peak was shallow, and he would sometimes cut it off if he was doing a photoshoot or movie. His mom actually dressed him in black slacks that were actually slacks! His blackshirt was a hard pressed button down with a pocket. His mom wouldn;t dare put any jewelry on him and he was always blinged out.

    She took the penny from her pocket and thought of numerous ways to add popping-copper to his ensemble! She thought of putting it at the top of the shirt pocket to adorn it as a copper button. She thought of putting it at the top of his slacks to adorn as a copper button. She thought it to be GROSS that she would think of touching her nephews pants; EEUGH!! Then she looked at his copper colored hand and tucked the penny into the slot of his fingers. She assumed the average corner boy wouldn't be paying that much attention. She was satisfied with her sacrifice to leave her European flat and see her nephew. She left the viewing room to find the women's restroom.

    TOOK came into the viewing room alone. He stood over ZING alone!! And the first thing he saw was the edge of a penny stuck between ZING's fingers. He pinched the coin by it's edge, because it was standing up and reached inside the pocket of his black shirt {button down with pocket} and deposited it. Guess they don't call him TOOK for nothing!

    He peered over his left shoulder once, then peered up and down every inch of Zing's corpse. His lips didn't move, but jealousy's private song, sang a whole non-verbal album! He was even envious because Zing switched to patent-leather Adidas. He presumed he should be the look-alike with the swaggiest sneakers. He still rocked the original Black Reeboks. He has an attitude because he was considered CUTE! ZING was considered FINE by the young girls! He never even thought that the name "LOOK-ALIKE" came from two biological brothers that LOOKED-ALIKE, although they were not TWINS.

Tooks sense of reasoning was blurred by a hate that kept him from seeing the brilliance of a leader that was able to brand a PHENOTYPE!! Zing taught Teacher the advantages in marketing their similarities, especially their facial features! Took thought of a few more reasons why Zing should be laying there and exited the viewing room before anyone else arrived. He, of course, knew the funeral home's layout and went out the back door where his car was.

A young girl from the Colfield area who ZING bought a backpack for; was helping her grandmother who babysat Zing, to get out of the car.

She noticed the man exiting the funerary as the guy who was shooting craps and every time he would roll a 7 or 11, he would chant, "We don't PLAY...in these fucking streets!" while he raked in his money!

The young girl had an eerie feeling about the guy coming out of the back door of a funeral home, but didn't know who she should tell. She minded her business and kept her mouth shut.

By now, Silh was re-entering the viewing area after braiding her own Pocahontas braids. She went again to view her nephew before the rest of the family was due to arrive. Surprisingly, she didn't notice the missing penny

143

right away, but when she did...she assured herself no one else was around. Then she looked in the lobby to see if anyone arrived early.

She saw through the glass a young girl holding two crutches in one hand and her grandmother's arm with the other. She held the door open for them and asked if they saw anyone else around the premises. The young girl didn't know the diva and kept her mouth shut. The grandma responded "NAHH sweetie!"

Silh quickly jumped outside the door to hold it from a position that wouldn't impede the two from entering.

She saw through the reflection, as she was holding the door that the other cars were pulling up in the parking lot behind her.

Just inside the lobby an usual thing occurred, the young girl hurried to give her grandmother the crutches then turned around and ran out the door and across the parking lot to grab Myona around the waist and give a kids version of "condolences." She hurried to tell what she saw to a woman who was like an aunt to her.

Myona asked Silh if she saw the guy Amelia was describing.

Silh asked, "What guy?" Amelia replied, "The cute guy with the bushy eyebrows. He has on BS3's with Classic Reeboks"

Myona said, "TOOK!"

Silh asked, "Who's TOOK?"

Myona in a sisterly type gossip unknowingly tells Silh all about Tooks position in Teacher's army, with emphasis on his jealousy towards ZING! She expounded on which of the 24 hr. shifts he managed. Wizzard's drug empire ran 8 hour shifts, and they ran drugs, exchanged products and personnel during the same shifts the authorities changed personnel; Took's management duties were from 11:00 PM through 7:00 AM. He rarely had to manage the 10 member crew because so many examples were demonstrated for mistakes, excuses, and slickery that his shift's creed or motto became "NO EXCUSES!!" Besides, many of their ex-workers were the ones who received 40 -.40's!! [R.I.P!!]

He wasn't as treacherous as Teach, but he definitely was responsible for a dozen funerals, half of which were at the funerary where Z was reposed.

Silh's decision to drive through the "M" was purely tactical. Based on the info her grieving sister provided, she knew this was the 3-11 shift she was observing. Nevertheless, she was beginning to understand the model her nephew used to acquire his empire. She was absolutely certain all his corners would be run like a franchise, because that's what they were taught at an early age.

She knew how her PISCEAN nephew thought. He would follow her father's franchising blueprint "DO RIGHT DO RIGHT, REPEAT!" He would surely repeat any successful business model. Not only would he repeat the success of his most profitable shift, he would repeat the model per each location he acquired. So she was able to deduce how the Colfield strip would be managed, minus the dice games.

Teacher was a stickler for ole school rules: "Don't get high on your own supply" etc. He forbade: saggy pants; profanity in front of seniors and children; open air crap games; public drug usage and impulsive displays of violence.

The mere fact that Took was seen and heard shooting dice AND openly using profanity in front of a minor, indicated a world of troubles within the ranks of the empire. Yet the most damaging and incriminating evidence that Took provided to incriminate himself was the exact words of the secret OATH the kin shared.

His knowledge and brashness of the oath added a whole new perspective on her nephew's demise. Just like a mirror image of Teach violating the family's order and creeds; Took was violating Teacher's orders and creeds.

She deduced that as ruthless and treacherous as Teach was regarding the family order; Took was as disrespectful and blatant, regarding Teacher's orders. So he would have violated the, "Don't kill each other's family" decree, and with impunity.

She concluded Took was as far off as his Teacher, he was heartless, soulless, and rule-less!

She could almost assume watching the guy at the "M" with the BS3's sniffing something up his nose, that these actions indicated a mutiny of some kind. It almost seemed like 'one apple spoiling the bunch,' or the crew learned mutiny by Teacher's example, she could almost assume.

Silh deduced: if Teach wasn't responsible for his brother's murder, someone would be looking for him next; or ...he, Took, and the other BS3 look-alikes were in cahoots about something.

Silh now felt that purveying the "M " was extremely fruitful surveillance, and it was time to cruise through Colfield.

*

Riding through the Coldspring and Dolfield=Colfield area, she noticed the 3-11 shift of BS3's was reckless and more or less, a banded unit of gangsters: one was shooting dice, another was making moves on a juvenile, one was visibly handing an addict something and another was nodding from something, probably PERCOCETS.

This shift was lawless, and could explain why Z was killed during this shift in this area. It appears, no one is watching anyone's back!

Next, she decided to see the site where her nephew was killed. From two blocks away, she could see numerous balloons and mementos at a specific tree. She knew from the gossip he'd taken refuge behind a tree when he was slain.

Closer up she could distinguish balloons, liquor bottles and teddy bears placed all around the tree.

She also noticed a whole slew of gigantic city-provided trash cans. She laughed at the size and noted they were large enough to put people in.

As she was riding past the site, she noticed atop the tree, the Twilight Star, boasting its many facets like a twinkling chandelier!

She didn't perceive it to be a sign, but it very well may have been. A flood of memories barged in of Popp's stories about the twilight star and she figured it was time to test some theories.

She recalled Teach telling a story when he knew it would be dark in 12 minutes because he saw the Twilight Star afloat the Cerulean Blue water. He was young and on the beach with his cousins when he decided to play magician. He actually had his cousins believing he made the darkness appear! She knew her nephew wasn't poetic nor would he speak phrases like that, no she knew it would've been something Popp taught.

She decided to test the theory. At the next corner, she searched til she found the star in the southern sky, because she looked left to spy a star, she kept straight to head west towards the sunset. In order to get the full effect of the theory, she went three parallel streets over to the main thoroughfare and continued west. There were intermittent splashes of shade and sunset as she traveled the westward road. By the time she reached the Milford Hills, the night was in her rearview mirror, indicating the truth to the theory. She was enlightened.

*

The 18th day after Zing's death, was the Autumnal Equinox. Not many people really knew, this day was the actual EQUINOX!!! WHY? The standard calendar tells you specific dates about solstices and equinoxes. However, Equimeans Equal; Nox - means Night, ...Oh well!!, ..you do the math!!

The weather was forecasted to be a perfect September day. It was already expected to be 77° at sunrise; 7:14 am. The rest of the day will proceed with low humidity, no clouds, and expected to be 77° when sun sets at 7:14 pm.

On this day it is believed that within a certain window of time a portal opens in our Solar System allowing Souls to enter and leave the planet unexplained. This day also signifies a pivotal point where energies, and polarities reverse.

Pisces: because their fish swim in opposite directions; are familiar with changing directions! Teach alternated his managers, as well as personnel, based on intel, or either 45 or 75 day intervals. Took was on the 3-11 in the Colfield territory. CARROT was stuck at Walbrook Junction. The twins QOQA and SOSA held down the "M". BLACKTOP managed the Southern regions below Pratt Street. JK, and SNOBBS, hadn't been assigned yet. A lot was going on, Tooks lady went into labor, and Teach, because all hands were on deck, stepped in to manage Colfield in Took's stead. Teach implemented baseball caps to the uniforms and with their mandatory masks for the pandemic being all black, you could barely tell anyone of the look-alikes from the other.

*

MYONA was conflicted!! she knew what the bloody taste in the back of her throat meant, however, she struggled with the tug in her HEART. If anyone else but her WIZTAMAN would've caused that taste of vengeance, they would've already been on the news confounding her weapon of choice (fingernail- needle) as the mystery weapon!

[*She loved the neat idea of the eardrum closing around the exit wound and presenting as earwax*]

Plus, she was so gorgeous she could get next to any target! Still, the confusion in her heart,  and the core of the creed she was raised on, won't allow her to snitch on her child, nor can she find it in her pedigree to raise her hand against her own seed.

She had a different father than the others and her father taught her that she was created by love, because he was in-love with her mother, and love will always be her POWER. So she superseded her woes and did what she was taught.

She headed for the sunrise at DRUID HILL PARK to release some tension; she had 44 minutes to make it!

Druid Heights has an eerie vibe!! Could this be the reason for the mysticism in this town? Could the energies from the days of the Druids, who the town was named after, be responsible for the esoteric occurrences? If they named the place after themselves, they certainly populated the joint!! Right? Could that explain the Barbarism in Murderland? What if, descendants of the Druids are scattered throughout the villages: Park Heights, EA, RNG, CBS, WLC, UPTON, GROVE, PENNORTH, possessing powers they don't know they have? Would that make a unique species go APESHIT when confronted with an overwhelming flood of emotions/powers they weren't trained to handle, but were GODSENT to manage, channel, and control? Would the species seek each other out and form a brotherhood? If so, they would probably gather around DRUID HILL PARK to do exercises of some kind on this day!

Maybe some Druids were at their eponymous park, doing things only Druids would do, but there was no news of any rituals or ceremonies reported from the concrete jungle.

She prepped in front of the MOORISH TOWER, facing ORION! Her father taught her the easy way to pray: "SCREAM!!!".

.40 Cal: "Her nephew was killed with one; and she didn't like it !!

*She remem...*

*" Sweetheart, there are lots of people who don't know how to pray! Think of all the creatures GOD made; do any of them go through any ritualistic incantations?" "NO!!, but they all scream, cry, or utter their needs to the universal GOD as they know it to be; don't they? So, we are gonna go to the top of this hill and send out our own version of harmonic expression to signify our cries and needs! We are gonna do it 3 times! The first one, will represent the voice for [the child in you that didn't have a voice] the PAST. The second, represents the voice of today's exasperations which warrant a delayed response; work, relationship, etc. [the adult that can't express or speakout at times] the PRESENT. The third, is to trailblaze a faithful path for the upcoming concerns, it represents your faithful, loving tone towards something you desire, that GOD will provide! {JEHOVAH JIREH - GOD PROVIDES} It has a different quality utterance from the frustration, or helpless scream; it's a thankful Praise for what GOD has already "DONE" that you haven't seen yet!!*

So Myona stood in the spot where her family usually screamed together and poured out her soul to the Universe. She hummed some, and screamed some, but heaving cries seemed to do the trick!

.40 Cal: "Her nephew was killed with one; and she didn't like it !!

*

On the last stop of his journey in Charlotte, N.C., SAINT awakened, shortly after daylight, to an auspicious type of dream. First, and foremost, the dream/vision was animated in

*cartoo...*

*There were very unique animals that represented the 5 elements: a long, skinny Elephant represented AEARTHERS; two-headed Eagle represented SUN; All White Peacock represented OCEANIA; See-through/black Eel represented DARK MATTER; and an INDIGO-colored, gelatinous creation of man represented THOUGHT.*

*Antinatural THOUGHTS from humans on planet, cause DARK MATTER to contract; which causes the SUN to flare through his nose and expand OCEANIA. This makes the INDIGOMAN who rides on the ELEPHANT perspire and become evil. And...without warning, permission, or justification, begin to execute anyone in his region who is unjust; PERIOD!! These,..are the rogue branch of the MALAKIM!! The roguest-est branch is color-blind, and they become irritated and incestuous; not murderous! during these regular flares. However, in extreme flares they will mass murder, rape, ravage, and eat, anyone who is unjust in their region!*

.40 Cal: "Her nephew was killed with one; and she didn't like it !!

This was only the second time he had a dream in cartoons. He really saw the power of the Angels this time and enjoyed the mind-movie, despite not having a clue to the riddle. He was a seasoned master and even taught the class on pulling the trigger, plus, he knew the CAUSAL PLANE was up to something if he received a colorfully animated transmission. So he practiced what he'd been preaching and believed the Universe 'has already DONE!!' whatever that mumbo jumbo meant!

He was excited to get back home and see his brood, even though he had 21 interviews to conduct about his YAZZING!

For TANEKA, it was business as usual. She didn't get visions, like the clairvoyants in the family, she was more clairaudient like her father first started. She'd hear her instructions, and do it! and she only dreamt when she had migraines. Usually, that would portend catastrophes like: tsunamis, hurricanes, earthquakes, etc. She had plenty of kills, but she didn't get picture-messages for her assignments; if something came to her, she just did it, no questions asked. She knew she didn't have beef with any of the people she slayed; so she figured the taste of vengeance must represent an enemy of ELOHIM. Therefore, she'd take another one for the team, as she often did, and slit someone's, anyone's throat for GP, just to send a message from the family that we require retribution for our blood, then ride back to Pennsylvania and get ready for work tomorrow.

*

Silh was in the yard doing her morning yoga. Her Spirit was still perplexed, even though she had been praying to keep from mourning. One nephew was dead, the other had issues of biblical proportions, and their mama was as distraught as EVE was when CAIN killed ABEL. Silh knew her sister believed 1000% in the family creed "We take care of our own!" However, when the culprit is your own seed, "Who do you get to take out the **trash;"can** I do it?"

Silh tried to discern whether or not it was her grief for Z, and her loyalty to their oath; her contempt for Teach, and his disdain for the family order; or her empathy for her oldest sister, with the pain and agony that seemed to motivate her vengeance.

She still hasn't attributed any of her urges to her ENOCHIAN pedigree, and she never figured out why she was taught the PATRIARCHS and their " begats"- [ *from ADAM >ENOCH >NOAH> ABRAHAM >DAVID, SOLOMON, >AFRICA>WEST INDIES > AMERICA*], nor does she realize her bloodline is from the Warrior

{MICHAEL}Human/Angels: MILCHIZEDEK/MALAKIM!! That's RIGHT!! SILH- is a HIT-ANGEL, AOD, and doesn't know it yet!! but she couldn't ignore the compulsion to settle the family's score, no matter who was responsible {GABRIEL}. She'd seen numerous other family members' "Take one for the team", and initiate the 'Execution of Judgment'{SHOFTIEL} on the perpetrators of their family's grief {ELOHIM'S enemies}, but she never had to read the streets and make an executive decision on what she deemed was the appropriate message to send to the streets. She heard on more than enough occasions, that it doesn't matter who goes down; just that, somebody answers for our blood!

That ends NOW!! {AZRAEL}, she decided! If Teach is gonna misuse the family creed to satisfy his own interpretations, then she was gonna personify her father's proverbs on another level; *"We take care of our own!! That's the creed, DONE!! The deed!!"* That's the exact, perfect message to send.

Just then, Silh had her first LUCID VISION {URIEL} while in her '**Warrior 2**' yoga pose.

In a few milliseconds, she *envis....*

*five animals experiencing weird metamorphoses: a see-through creature expanded to the fullness of space and disappeared into dark matter, all that was left was the guts of the beast, which turned out to be the Cosmos; another creature turned green like grass and became the color green around the entire globe, then merged into the harddrive of the EARTH, and became*

156

*the THOUGHTS of the planet; one beast, came from the dust and returned to the dust; another came from the air and returned to its origin; a man came from the water and returned to the waters!*

Although *dream-interpretation* was the weakest of her spiritual gifts, she pulled the trigger of faith and believed GOD had already "DONE" whatever the obscure, esoteric picture-language OLOGIZED that HE'D "DONE!!" And faster than instantly - like millisecondly, a volt went through her body, or in her body, or whatever the heck happened!! She didn't jerk or flinch or in no way acknowledge the rainbow that just indwelled her; she was oblivious to what the Heavenly Host considered to be obedience and its greater rewards!

Silh had a tight schedule with a specific itinerary!! She was late to the fancy Athletic Center, and when she arrived, a homeless lady was pacing outside "Speaking in Tongues". Silh deduced this was the timing of KAIROS, and the Demonstration to her Confirmation/Vision, which she also didn't comprehend, but remembered her father mentioning something about: Confirmation, Demonstration, and Manifestation, or some combination of three things occurring from the time you believe until the time of manifesting WHATEVER you believe! Today, she intended to believe every foreign language she didn't comprehend, and she was gonna apply herself in meditation, or in lucid dreaming, to ask her Highest Self to change her way of thinking so that she could comprehend these mysteries and for CLARITY to intuit what the anointed woman was saying or meaning.

157

.40 Cal: "Her nephew was killed with one; and she didn't like it !!

After the gym, she wanted to double-check her intel before her conscience could accept what her urges were driving her towards. She had the HEART, the skill, the stealth, but had never been tested. This is a different motivation, EVErything in her BEing was telling her that this is her score to settle, and she intends for it to be a different outcome!! Immediately, she noticed an attitude of determination that, until now, hadn't surfaced!

[*The Archangel TZADKIEL - Angel of RIGHTEOUSNESS, indwelled her for this mission, and for responding to the call of HIGHER PURPOSE. She had already naturally invoked several of the 12 'Angels of Vengeance' without even knowing, or trying, but by the* **choices** *she was making! If she invokes the rainbow of 7 Archangels,* (by choosing highest, purest, altruistic attitudes) *she will manifest the PRESENCE OF ELOHIM on EARTH, and with the righteous attitudes emerging, it seems likely!*

*Actually, the angels were double-checking her HEART, to see if she would waiver, or proceed with their guided urges; they truly tend to favor guts, courage, balls,...* **HEART!!**

*Some Angel language transmitted to human language is inverted, sorta like the left-brain; right-body MYSTERY. If you've never askt yourself where "QUESTIONS" come from, perhaps, it's Angels, trying to tell you something!!* {***THE ANSWER IS IN THE QUESTION!!***}

Somebody, anybody took a just, and righteous soul from this planet; and it stirred up things inside of this humangel that had her contemplating murder sprees.

Somebody, anybody took a young holy angel from their mission before their appointment, and it was searing a disdain for mankind deep down in the embers of her heart!

Somebody, anybody took her nephew, and she didn't like it! And she is not having it!! And in this moment's decision, she's definitely DETERMINED to avenge her nephew!!

WHEW!! She quickly started to lower the zipper to give her hot-flashed body a breeze {URIEL-*"FIRE of GOD " indwelled* }. Then, she tried to control her "thoughting!" She was extremely HOTT!! about the unmitigated temerity of anyone to alter GOD'S purpose, and she got even hotter! Once the quick balls of sweat started to surface, she immediately clenched her teeth, and became irritated.

She wanted to righteously kill everyone involved!

For the first time, she experienced what so many others before her had discovered about the taste of blood that floods the throat and tongue when you're so wrathful {SAMMAEL} that you feel like you can take on 100 soldiers. Their bloodline took the sign to mean it was time to hit your mark if one was delivered into your hands! Either way, Silh was pissed off to the highest pisstivity, and needed to soothe the savage beast raging inside her. She stretched, cardio-ed, and maxed out her lifting weights, and still the urges didn't subside.

[*If she included the 10,000 steps anticipated to be walked before the day's end, it was destined to be a busy day, and she hoped to be drunk and exhausted for the flight home. She had a small window of time before she had to meet the girls at 3pm., and her partner- manager asked her to stop by the club before she left the States.*]

The Gentlemen's Club opened at noon and Tierra was wiping the bar when the BO$$ came in. She ushered her over to the corner table to share the news she acquired. Once seated, Tierra says, "Gurlll guess what happened here last night?"

Just then, Shanel walked in, dropped her bag on the bar, and as she was racing to the restroom, hollered back, what yall talking bout? Tierra shouted, "That dumb shit from last night!" She shouted through the bathroom door, " Gurlll, guess what happened up in here last night Babay? Wait a minute, let me narrate the story."

She exited the bathroom sniffling. She wiped her nose thoroughly. She came from the back, making gestures indicative of a griot.

" As the music played in a dimly lit, second floor, privacy-glass walled, exquisitely kept Gentlemen's club, she demonstrated how WOOT sashayed towards the sexy managers, to offer a drink with a corny swag. He didn't know they were the managers, and was too toasted to recognize them if he did know them.

**They were truly sexy too!** They both wore "SILHOUETTE" brand Catsuits. These were the creations that started two trends:

1) Women wearing colours in the shades of their complexions, despite the business making as many colours as lipsticks; and

2) Women NOT wearing chic, multi-colored catsuits before twilight.

This NUDE - effect trend, with the Designer's brilliance, looked like body-art, in some styles, and Alien attire in others. It really added to the sex appeal of Cougars and seniors with awesome bodies.

They used a patented fabric, and named it **Gjishel**. The denure's elasticity perfectly accented asses like onions.

However, the Fashion trend was booming, and catsuits were leading the way!

**TIERRA** - wore an Almond colored sample with copper colored collar and cinched ankles. Because of her Honey colored complexion, the combo of colors presented as NUDE at first glance. Tierra's curls were auburn with copper colored streaks, and whose head doesn't turn to see that sexy Goddess?.. NUDE?..WHEW!!

**COOKIE** wore a sample that was all black with slits at the thighs, and one up the back. The collar and cinch were pewter-colored. Her pecan colored skin was on display through the slits. Cookie's hair was cut in a short style, colored black with pewter streaks. You'd really have to see it in person to appreciate the artistry.

Anyway, Woot asks, "What's yall's names"? Tierra, quick on her feet utters, "TIFFANY."! Cookie, a tad bit MYSTICAL on her feet, in a sultry voice, leans towards him with a whispering tone, says, "*SILHOUETTE*!" Still being corny and drunk, Woot asks, " How'd you get a name like that?" Nevermind, it's the club's name, as he was swaying back and forth while he looked around the venue. Already expecting the dumbass question, she retorts, "If I tell you...Oh,..nevermind." He was too inebriated to catch the buzz.

The girls looked at each other and knew exactly what the other was thinking. Cookie used the proximity of her boobs to navigate the moron to the inside of the corner booth as both women flanked him and ordered more drinks.

Cookie gave Tierra the eye to start the phishing expedition. Tierra knew if she mentioned the finest woman from that area, Woot would tell everything he hated about her man. He was a hater like that.

.40 Cal: "Her nephew was killed with one; and she didn't like it !!

The finest chick in his hood is DOMINIQUE - the nephew's girl.

Tierra said she liked nephew's fashions, Woot expressed dislike! She mentioned Dominique, he told everything he heard in the streets about why and how your nephew expired."
This serendipitous info gave them what she needed to fuel her fire!

*

Saint finished journaling the lord's PRESENCE in the "BOOK OF LIFE": which contains people's personal names, along with the onomastics of the names {*believed to be encounters with human angels (*Who dare NOT, could NOT, would NOT, believe they were angels) *of the 144,000 Elect*}

It also revealed places {*believed to be Sacred*}; and chronicled breathtaking psychic experiences that continue to happen {*believed to be sagas, dramas, or situations orchestrated by GOD, for SAINT to disclose to the "FERVENT PRAYOR, through FERVENT PRAYING" the onomastics of their name to REVEAL their hidden PURPOSE, and that they are members of the 144,000 Elect of The Most High GOD; accountable for 5,000,000 prayers towards the 1 Trillion Prayer Covenant*}; where the Author documented the mysterious occurrences regarding the symbiosis of a man and his GOD! Plus, he journaled sagas confirming GOD'S PRESENCE, and how GOD honored the Original Millisecond Covenant where ELOHIM kept HIS WORD by having KAIROS, and CHRONOS create the most AMAZING COINCIDENCES to assist Saint to pray fervently for mankind's putrid choices and their consequential results, which lead to the planet's turmoils.

Furthermore, these scenarios provide invaluable opportunities for Saint to be the first man credited with praying 1 Trillion self initiated prayers for the sagas mankind created by his choices! {ADAM-EVE; CAIN-ABEL; AZAZEL- SEMYAZA, etc.} Even if he has to live 127 years to do it!!

The short plane ride was only 2 hours. Saint put the journal away, and quickly slipped into a dreamy world. It didn't take long at all, before the cartoon characters started

*emerg...*

*An Eagle ate his own face! A mule turned into a Giraffe! A gelatinous creature merged into the intelligence of the Earth, and downloaded all the information in the Earth's harddrive, then expanded out of everyone's sight to the edge of the cosmos!!*

*The lucid dream revealed the same vibrations and energies from the Santa Fe experience, only this time, he recognized the surge penetrating his flesh, and woke up! This second animated vision assured him something meaningful was happening, and despite not knowing what the hell it meant, believed the Will of ALMIGHTY GOD {EL SHADDAI} would manifest!!*

.40 Cal: "Her nephew was killed with one; and she didn't like it !!

So, even in a lucid state, he did what he trained his subconscious mind to do - "SQUEEZE THAT TRIGGER" on FOREIGN languages!! You never know when you're entertaining an ANGEL!!!

*

Silh plotted to gather more intel by suggesting that a minion on the a.m. shift, happened to be very handsome, as she indulged Myona and Myesha at the waterfront restaurant RUSTY SCUPPER before her flight. It's expensive, but the cheapest expense to get done, what she was trying to get done! And, have two 100's drop her off at the airport, 3 hours before her International Flight; at 9:03 pm. The women informed her of all they knew about the morning shift, and who was scheduled.

Her strategy was to determine who would be on the 3- 11 shift by eliminating the personnel from the other two shifts; at the same time, misleading the ladies into thinking her interest was elsewhere. This process of elimination will help focus on the relevant look-alikes and figure out where the culprit wasn't! Actually, she was beyond infuriated and had already put together a time-frame, and frankly didn't give a damn right now about 5 of those S.O.B. 's, so she didn't give a shit about which one was gonna get it!! Except, she knew some of the minions were clueless, as well as innocent, based on Woot's report! And, since she familiarized herself with Colfield, that's where she'll concentrate her efforts; as long as no innocents were sitting

165

in Captain's chairs, which she doubted, she'd be able to live with herself once the deed was done! Silhouette was so serious about responding to her ancestors' call. They were urging her to answer the taste of blood on her tongue, representing her ancestors' blood which was spilt!!

[*Silhouette already reviewed the layout with Google Earth; gathered intel from everyone she could imagine; clocked po-po's locale, or lack thereof; charted the get-away into the night; checked the functionality of all operating equipment! and headed to Colfield.*]

The first person she observes as she cruises up Colfield has on, in addition to BS3's: police style sun shades; an all-black mask; and a floppy hat in the predawn hour; and is pacing up and down the block!! She became titillated, believing the only person 'that' eccentric would be her nephew! And GOD was sanctioning his unrighteous ass to get his just rewards!! She came close to getting "big headed", and began salivating when she started to "thought' how ea..", and quickly pulled the trigger to co-create "Allow me to be the instrument through which YOU fulfill YOUR PLAN, ELOHIM!! ÄMEN!!

Her eyes were quickly focused on the downturned, brand new, City-provided, 30-gal., trash can 80 feet away!! It was roughly 2 feet from the bushes; next to the 4 concrete steps in back of the house that owns a tree with lots of deflated balloons!!

.40 Cal: "Her nephew was killed with one; and she didn't like it !!"

She continued up the block, out of sight, and abruptly turned into the alley to come back down in front of the house with the fallen receptacle and use the airway between the two houses to reach the container! Of course, her logical mind couldn't make sense of the trash can, but knowing "ELOHIM is relentless in REVELATIONS", she intends to do as she was shown!

There were even more bushes around front and another trash can with the address painted in white was standing half-full with only a newly deposited black trash bag; she placed her quickbag atop the trash, and pulled down the other mask.

She was able to push the tail of the bike between the front bushes and the house; while leaving just a piece of rubber handle extended out into the airway for quick recovery!

She was about to get elated and remembered to stay humble and accept her role as ELOHIM'S instrument! She changed her paradigm by submitting to GOD'S WILL!!

Though the nerves didn't subside, her overstanding increased enough for her to envision a mission accomplished!!

She put on her gloves with the utmost determination to fulfill her purpose on this planet no matter what the "call", or who the vic, and right now, her attitude is "Whoever the fugck is representing these abominations [*she didn't know she knew that word??*] is about to get croaked!!! And she had a flight to catch! She scheduled her father's flight so she knew what time his plane would arrive. Her plan was to execute her family's cancer and be on the plane to Europe by the time her father returned!

She had no problem sliding behind the opposite landscape and peeping through the bushes to behold her taste of blood from her new vantage point next to the back steps. For a brief moment, she didn't think she would need the fallen container because the bushes provided such shelter. However, all the maneuvering it's taking to get under the brush and into the vessel proves challenging enough!

Before she exited from beneath the bushes, she extended her right arm to grasp the container's handle. It was simple to create the illusion that the can hadn't moved by dragging it slowly; very slowly! Then she reversed her leg position to thread, first, her left leg, then her right leg into the open end of the receptacle facing the mulch at the end of the step. She was actually able to sit on her butt, facing her target, covered by the bushes on her right, and the steps on her left. She used her left hand to pull the handrail for leverage to sit-up.

To her, the advantage was perfect. She was ready to run across the lawn in thirteen seconds and get it over with! But the vision urged her to enter into the trashcan the way she climbed into pillowcases when she was young. She dare not go Mary-contrary now! She held her breath like she was going underwater and dipped down into the container. She must've pleased ELOHIM, because she totally forgot she was claustrophobic, and instantly oozed into another lucid vision where she quickly pierced the adversary's medulla oblongata, 5 times, with an ice-pick!

Although it was only a Millisecond, *she envis...*

*The shade from the setting sun cast its image over the house, the bushes, the receptacle, and all the other neighbor's houses on the west side of the street. This seemed to add double darkness to her hideout.*

*She peered through the bushes like an owl, fixated on her prey, and its mannerisms. At one point, she became so focused that she thought time slowed down to show her the stealthiest path. In the blink of an eye, she envisioned herself crouched down low; behind his back, lower than his shoulders; aligned with his spine, and moving swiftly, directly towards her unsuspecting target. It felt so surreal, she knee-jerk false-started and caught herself, and took a breath to recalibrate! She hears familiar voices, he's on the phone, she emerges, black cat across the street scurries! She reaches for the 40 cal. He's oblivious to the incredibly stealthy Eagle about to sink her talons into his fairytale-life in the quiet little neighborhood. She practiced stealth, so her moves were seamless as well as soundless when she was within inches of her mark. Then she pulled the ice pick from within her pre-adjusted Citizens flex band and with expert precision shoves 3 of the 5 inches into his medulla oblongata twice before he dropped the phone on the*

169

*edge of the neighbor's grass just inside the pathway. In a feat of irony, he fell in the square of the walkway, next to the leaning Oak tree in an identical chalk line of her nephew. She quickly thrust the ice pick through his eardrum.*

It didn't take long before the close quarters caused her temperature to rise; The moisture arising from the heat was starting to make her skin clammy and before she allowed the perspiration to reach full blast, she became aware of her pedigree and the forces working inside of her being, and her internal forces started a fight with her conscious forces to return to reality and the task at hand.

Now she's really confused about which of the 3 visions she was to execute! Instantly, the receptacle stood up! When it did, her reflexes popped her out of the container like a circus game. She bee-lined towards the center of his spine, staying low, and zigging each time he would zag as he romanced on the cell phone.

The first sound heard was a twig cracking as she dashed across the manicured lawn! The next was: fwooph, ooghh, snap, crack, pulap, dadoomph, thoomp!!!

She pushed him away from her as if he was a jokester! Then quickly pivoted to walk across the lawn, pretending as if they were young lovers, pushing and shoving.

It worked so well, nobody saw the poetry of the prophetic fall, not even the prophetess, as she changes in the airway and scoops the bike! Her exit was so swift; she never noticed where he fell!

The dirt bike she boarded was typical in that area, the fact that it was blacked out was even more common. Once she tucked her ponytail beneath the helmet; put ZING'S lightweight puffed out jacket over her gloved hands; she was perfectly camouflaged from head to foot with Zing's Nike boots clicking the gears as she took off heading up Colfield towards the Western sunset.

As it was quickly growing dark in the East, a carload of goofballs were joyriding in the West. They were switching lanes up the thoroughfare, one of them climbed out the car window and sat on the door as the car was zooming up the street. When he saw the dirtbike up ahead in the left lane, he started shouting obscenities. Silh originally thought it may have been some retaliatory homeboys coming to avenge the fallen. Then the heckler continued shouting and reaching out towards the bike as if he wanted to grab the rider, and when he missed, he aimed at her with his two fingers and shouted "Forty Cal, bitch!!"

She assumed, with the timing and the weirdness of the act, that it must be a foreign language associated with the confirmation, demonstration stuff. So she squeezed the trig to accept whatever GOD had planned in this manifestation, and the millisecond she acknowledged the disdain from the heckler, the clutch on the bike popped and the vehicle went up in the air.

.40 Cal: "Her nephew was killed with one; and she didn't like it !!

While still in shock from the other two, obvious PRESENCES, her hands fell to her side with perfect balance to sustain the dirtbike at 12 O' Clock!! The amazing feeling sweeping over her consciousness opened her mind up like a panoramic movie screen. She had never experienced anything that could remotely be accounted as bliss, but this Heavenly state of attitude, and freedom like flying can only mean one thing!!

She had NO FEAR!! And maintained perfect PEACE!! While the *Milliseconds* made the 36 second Miracle seem to last memorably.

Somewhere inside the moment when the bike resurrected, the penny formerly wedged in her change pocket rolled out onto the asphalt where it took total advantage of the swift incline to boogie down Liberty road with serious ambition!! It didn't let the splinter of glass knock it off its purpose-driven course either!! Nope! It jumped over that shard like a high school hurdler; but the edge of the pothole proved to be a gamechanger for this ambitious piece of copper! The new direction aimed the penny towards the Mall's entrance, while it picked up momentum. It dinged a steel pipe and ricocheted back out into traffic. It weaved a few cars, and SUV's; then used all the forces exerted onto it to turn the first corner where the wind from a passing tractor trailer caused the penny to splat, right in the middle of the yellow lines that separate the lanes. The facedown penny found rest at the intersection of Liberty and Security Blvd.

During this small window of the Cerulean sky, various posts began to circulate throughout social media. HURTER INC posted some of the gruesome carnage that took place in such a small window of time.

Throughout the city, flashes of light were popping up like fireworks. Over Pratt St., a yellowish orb, shaped like a chariot hovered 50 feet in the air for all eyes to see the transubstantiation of a human into a ball of fire. Folks began to wonder if the ENOCHIANS returned?

At the Junction, orange follicles of hair landed on peoples faces as they blew/flew through the neighborhood. The explosive Spontaneous human combustion which blew/flew orange hair throughout Walbrook Junction was so powerful, fragments of flesh were found hanging from a tree in the county. A pawn shop on the East-side received his gold tooth! a snotty-nosed little kid wanted $10 to buy a stolen bike!

A man at the gas station just outside of Pennsylvania, had his throat slit by a man riding by on a Ninja cycle!

Another person dressed in all black attire was discovered in an alley next to the hospital downtown. He apparently had been stabbed several times in the back of his head!

The "M" had the most spectacular display of carnage! At the "M", one twin accused the other of pretending to be his twin brother and screwed his girl. Sosa killed Qoqa as soon as the Sun declined. He used a .40 Cal. When the indigo- colored blood poured from his head, it formed a rope-like cord and

173

raced to the sewer drain, where it turned green as it got closer to water. There were limbs that originated there, strewn as far off as Mondawmin Mall. Vomited bone fragments aligned West-side streets, confusing officials as to where the deposits were coming from. Some speculated, the culprit must have wings!!

Seventy feet above the mini-mart at Colfield, blazed a purplish gelatinous orb that seemed to be made of an unknown material. It appeared to be like liquid glass on fire. Intermittently, huge balls of goo, the size of watermelons, dropt to the ground and broke into millions of b-b sized balls and rolled throughout the community until sundown when they grew feet like ants, and bored themselves into the core of the Earth! On the ground beneath the orb lay a gemstone with a copper splat melted onto it!

So, on one of the only two days of the year with 12 hours of day, and 12 hours of night; the last image of the day, and first image of the night that was captured across the hills of *MILFORD MILLS*, amidst the Cerulean Twilight, was a SILHOUETTE, of a biker {ON-12...with NO HANDS!!}

Next, someone uploaded a video on INSTAGRAM of a Silhouette of a biker {ON-12!; NO HANDS!!} going over Milford Hills at sundown!
Another person uploaded a different video of a silhouette of a biker {ON-12...PONYTAIL}going over Pikes Hills at sundown! Then, believe it or not, a third video was uploaded of a silhouette of a biker {ON-12...FRENCH BRAIDS waving a .40 Cal.}going over Reisterstown Hills!

.40 Cal: "Her nephew was killed with one; and she didn't like it !!

*

At the end of this auspicious day, Myona pulled into the slotted parking space provided for her townhome. From 36 ft. away, she noticed a corrugated tray made out of a box that was used for sodas. It appeared to have 3 full McDonald's bags and one handled McDonald bag on the makeshift tray. She assumed the kids were in there having so much fun, they didn't hear UBEREATS. If they didn't notice they were hungry, she wasn't going to remind them. She managed to get in the house with the food, without anyone noticing. She made it upstairs to kick off her shoes and drop her purse, go to the bathroom, and then see what they ordered. She sat on the side of the bed and grabbed the shortest bag. Inside was a message written on a torn piece of brown paper bag, "With all due respect, ' We take care of our own' this is the .40 Cal. that killed your son!!"

The room began to turn gray, her head started to spin! Even though she was sitting down, her knees got weak and she slid off the side of the bed. The last thing she remembered  hearing was ".40 Cal." and a wave of shock paralyzed her reality. As the shutter to her consciousness was closing in, her mind recorded one last sound - dadoomph, thoomp!!

**THE END** *{deed is DONE!!}*

.40 Cal: "Her nephew was killed with one; and she didn't like it !!

**EPILOG:** This creation and its sequels, prequels, or spin-offs is intended to attract **CARLA HAYDEN, JADA PINKETT SMITH, TYLER PERRY, OPRAH WINFREY or any** philanthropist interested in improving the quality of life for single mothers and their lineage.

We're asking these benefactors primarily, to acquire rights {$11,111,111.11 as a contribution to

**FOUNDATION FOR SINGLE MOTHERS**

**A subsidiary of EloKim Holdings LLLP** to make donations wherewith to create an operation to distribute life-changing assets (cars, houses, etc,) to a red-lined demographic, so that their sweat equity is not just for items, rather it will be to promote a better quality of life for their heirs.

The proceeds from this publication will be used to fund FOUNDATION FOR SINGLE MOTHERS!

*Whenever, wherever, or however this material finds you, proves*

*evidence of a very important **TRUTH!***

***YOU attracted it to your SACRED presence! for a Sacred***

***reason!***

.40 Cal: "Her nephew was killed with one; and she didn't like it !!

*Yes! Your network was instrumental in the procurement of this manifestation, but the true GRANTOR of all BLESSINGS (such as this one) knows the secrets you need, for the version of trials and tribulations you face.*

*Maybe you attract falsehood and illusion and don't know why; you would attract a document of this caliber {excuse the pun}.*

*You may be desiring to comprehend the mysteries of Laws of Attraction; again, there may be a message here.*

*You may have the kind of power that causes whatever you speak to occur, but you keep saying dumbass shit out your mouth, and when it happens you blame everyone else but yourself! You have the wrong concept of yourself.*

*You are more HOLY, SANCTIFIED, & SACRED than you believe. Being more Holy, more Sanctified, and more Sacred than you believe means you have a bond with GOD, and didn't get the memo. Regardless of what you believe HIS HOLY metric to be, HIS part of*

.40 Cal: "Her nephew was killed with one; and she didn't like it !!

*the Covenant bonds your WORDS as a prophet or prophetess, priest or priestess, regardless whether you see yourself the way HE sees you or not. A bonded word will manifest by GOD'S POWER, regardless of the speaker's conscientiousness. That means if you keep saying dumbass shit, and it keeps happening, YOU...are the cause! You are Special/ Chosen/Anointed, in the eyes of GOD, but you didn't get the memo of your pedigree, and don't have a clear understanding of the ramifications of your dumbass statements.*

*Let's be clearer, even fussing your dumbass out, and using words like "dumbass" to do it, doesn't negate the Sanctity or Holiness of either party. Rather, this represents the intolerance of a powerful, yet ignorant, demographic of people {144,000} who don't know they are thee most Spiritually powerful people on the planet. So if urban dialect mixed with Spirituality causes a stumbling block for you, this material may not be able to penetrate the delusions of how and where GOD works.*

.40 Cal: "Her nephew was killed with one; and she didn't like it !!

*Change the paradigm of your context, and start to speak life in situations and circumstances, regardless if you feel like you are calling it like you see it, or believe you are telling it like it is. **SPEAK-LIFE!** You'll be gratified to manifest your soul's desires through positively spoken statements.*

.40 Cal: "Her nephew was killed with one; and she didn't like it !!

# OLOGIES & ONOMASTICS

The OLOGIES in reference here are not like the American definitions meaning "the study of", but rather the Greek summation of "speaks"!

Muddle through your entire vocabulary and focus on words ending in "OLOGY", then substitute the meaning of the suffix "the study of" with the summation of the suffix "speaks" to change the paradigm of common words into a spellbinding and life-changing language that will enhance your daily outlook, and enrich the meaning of your own ONOMATOLOGY -{human being's **NAMES** speak}.

Create new meanings like: ASTROLOGY- "stars speak"; NUMEROLOGY- numbers speak; GEOLOGY- Earth speaks; GENEALOGY- DNA speaks, ONOMATOLOGY- names speak, THEOLOGY- GOD SPEAKS, COSMOLOGY- cosmos speaks, etc., to broaden your perspective of how the Universe is "speaking" to you!!

.40 Cal: "Her nephew was killed with one; and she didn't like it !!

Few have advanced to reach this level of Divine interpretation; therefore, this information is seeking the 144,000 ELECT to awaken and enlighten them for the purpose of bringing the Light of the MOST HIGH to this planet using the language of ANGELOLOGY {angels speak}. This is not an easy course to undergo, it's a mandatory course for the ELECT of the MOST HIGH! Somewhere beyond the DIVINE saga in the garden, the idea of mankind was intended to evolve into human/angelkind!

You may scoff, and under your breath, dismissively murmur, "Yeah,..what the heck?"; but you can't deny the possible intentionality of the signs we've already seen. Namely, the entity you are at this present stage was once: A THOUGHT, a Vision, an Attraction, a Vibration, an Intercouse, a sperm/egg, an embryo, a fetus, a newborn, an infant, a toddler, a child, a prepubescent, a teen, an adult; and then what, all of a sudden the intentionality **STOPPED?** Let's NOT be naive!

.40 Cal: "Her nephew was killed with one; and she didn't like it !!

Continue to pay attention to the plethora of **SIGNS** and **SYMBOLS** all around you, and it will become clear. There's more being shown, than what we're seeing; and way more being said, than what we're hearing.

Look to see; Listen to hear, and with diligence and practice, you too, will be comprehending the voice of the Cosmos and the various styles in which it speaks.

ONOMASTICS or ONOMATOLOGY is one of the "OLOGIES" the Cosmos uses to spell out purposeful sentences using people's names, and the names of places and things they've experienced, just like it was in biblical days. This could include, but not be limited to names of : addresses, jobs, schools, teachers, friends, enemies, cities, states, countries, and organizations, which are all interpretable symbols. Unfortunately, interpreting the Universal-SYMBOLOGY {symbols speak} will be as unintelligible and incomprehensible as an average American learning: Calculus, Physics, Sanskrit, or Chinese. Every new, secondary, or tertiary language requires : time, practice, and translation. Interpreting the LIVING WORD, which is

.40 Cal: "Her nephew was killed with one; and she didn't like it !!

exactly what you'd be doing, is much like DREAM interpretation, but instead of the symbols needing the interpretation being in 2 dimensional - image form, the symbols you'll be interpreting will be in 3 dimensional - natural form; real!!

The NAME of each person, place or thing, the Universe has placed in your consciousness, spells out a meaningful statement to your HIGHER-SELF to interpret and attempt to translate to your conscious mind through Intuition. So, please, please, please pay attention to what the angels are guiding your eyes to see, and your ears to hear!!

If you exuded a need to comprehend the incomprehensible, or fathom the unfathomable, and a copy manifested, you have a special kind of power to summon this or any other material to your presence. If so, then you prove the point above, that you are powerful; and these Fables may give you additional KEYS to deduce your grand PURPOSE, and secure your DESTINY on this or any planet!

.40 Cal: "Her nephew was killed with one; and she didn't like it !!

## SOME KEYS ARE in THESE FABLES!!

Nevertheless, YOU!! Are still the impetus which created the majic - *which caused the network to be instrumental in the procurement of this manifestation*! Majical timing has occurred; and it has nothing to do with any chance, circumstance, or any force outside of your control. Nor can the serendipity be attributed to luck or happenstance since we are simultaneously exchanging the majic right now!

The POWER is YOU!!

# YOUR THOUGHTS!

Your thoughts are the most crucial currency creating the circumstances {opportunities to demonstrate your degrees of FAITH, or lack thereof, when you pray} that determine the daily events happening to you or for you.

You may have heard speeches about "the power of thought" from a NEW-AGE GURU; or perhaps you've read a tabloid suggesting the possibility of controlling the events in your life with positive thinking. Maybe in the circles you travel, people have mentioned the experience of co- creating. Either way, the CREATOR of our Universe, sent YOU a MEMO in the language indigenous to our Cosmos!

The reading of this material is no mere coincidence. The WORDS are alive! They speak guidance and resolution to the current conundrums you're facing.

The SPIRIT of the prayer which compels this composition is the consciousness which created the Heavens and the Earth. That consciousness knows you and the other 143,999, and seeks you as diligently as your thoughts seek answers from the Universe.

To find an answer to life's questions is to satisfy the soul with a quenching refreshment. Discovering this material is the worthwhile, quenching evidence of some recent and fervent changes in your

.40 Cal: "Her nephew was killed with one; and she didn't like it !!

THOUGHTS/PRAYERS!! ***ONLY GOD KNOWS!!*** Perhaps this material brought that KEY which you summoned!

Accept the fact that you are the POWER, and have always been the power creating your situations. The LAW OF ATTRACTION which brought this material to you is limitless and will bring all your Rightly guided thoughts to MANIFESTATION.

In this artform, be it novel or poem, pour your bottomless imagination into the Universe of Prophetic Words and allow GREAT SPIRIT to shape your thoughts and environment, and enjoy the artform for its creative simplicity for depicting the challenges in the Cosmos with everyday characters; as well as its esoteric profundity for choosing Spiritual technologies to resolve everyday challenges.

You will experience a vicarious joy-ride through the Highly responsible eyes of a Theurgist; ELOHIM'S ELECT. You'll feel the majic which speaks to ONE situation- speaks to multiple situations around the globe!

.40 Cal: "Her nephew was killed with one; and she didn't like it !!

May you find answers in your questions, joy in your tears, laughter in your sorrow, FAITH in your doubts, and wisdom in your folly!!

If no human ever spoke LIFE to you:

# BE COMPLETE!

.40 Cal: "Her nephew was killed with one; and she didn't like it !!

# Summary

A catsuit- wearing, ponytail- slinging, AUNT!!! avenges her nephew's murder.

Business suit by day, catsuit by night, Cherokee {a self-made Fashionista} summons the Malakim to affect her ultimate goal...

## REVENGE!!

# For her sister's child!

She fancied a poetic justice where his killer would be slain in the same spot where her nephew was found!

www.ingramcontent.com/pod-product-compliance
Lightning Source LLC
Chambersburg PA
CBHW061207170626
46809CB00003B/1273